The Beach

Including the Novella, *Short Time*

Jaye Frances

Books by Jaye Frances

World Without Love – The Series
A Suspense Thriller Trilogy including:
Betrayed
Reunion
Redemption

∼

The New Girl in Town
And Other Journeys Above and Below the Belt

∼

The Beach
Featuring the novella, *Short Time*

∼

The Kure

∼

Love Travels Forever

The Beach

Redstone Press Media

ISBN 978-0692541906

Printed in the United States of America

www.JayeFrances.com

The Beach

Short Time

To that lovely strip of sand and sea,
Where we walk hand-in-hand,
Just you and me . . . .

One

The Descending Horde

The breeze was too warm for a sweater and the water too cold for swimming.

Useless weather, he thought. *Good for nothing.*

The mild transition between spring and summer didn't appeal to Alan. He was already missing the winter seas and the raw, wet air that hurt your lungs if you drew it in too fast. In spite of his disfavor with the calendar, he still had the beach and today it was just the way he liked it—empty, not another soul for as far as he could see. The beach was his church, and he worshipped best alone.

He walked at a slower gait than usual, taking it all in, knowing that within a few weeks the crowds would return, littering the sand with their ice cream wrappers and cigarette butts, and contaminating the clean, salty air with the ear-stench from a hundred black and silver boom-boxes bought on sale from the local drug and notions.

Several summers ago he had tried to teach them, to show them how their seasonal invasion, their thoughtlessness and stupidity, was damaging the beach and the wildlife that lived there. They had responded with blank expressions and glassy-eyed indifference, some arrogantly turning up their radios to drown him out, to push him out of earshot.

As bad as the tourist-filled days were—so bad he never ventured outside in the afternoon—the evenings were far worse. That's when he found his precious beach wounded and bleeding, the sand punctured with empty beer cans and still-glowing cigar stubs. Even more vulnerable, the higher dunes were frequently left suffocating in tons of grease paper, used Kleenex, and the occasional disposable diaper—damning evidence that raging human scum had fucked his beach.

One night, after trying to diffuse his anger with a fifth of Johnnie Walker Red, he had admitted the truth—if only to himself: He would kill them if he could. Club them with the very same shovel he used to pile up their wretched trash, and then let the birds pick their bones.

He pushed the thought from his mind. They would be here soon enough. Right now, he had the beach to himself, and he would savor the solitude for a couple more days, maybe a week, depending on this useless weather.

Alan was taking his usual late afternoon walk along the shoreline. As he inhaled the salt-laden mist and felt the tightly-packed sand crunch under his feet, he easily imagined the light breeze at his back gently urging him toward a large outcropping of exposed granite at the south end of the strand.

As he covered the final hundred yards separating him from the rocky projection, he slowed his pace. No matter how many times he saw it, he couldn't help but appreciate the enduring strength of the weather-worn monolith. Dark and craggy, it was an unremarkable monument. But for Alan, its stubborn and defiant stand against the elements gave it character and personality, and he always approached it with a kind of pantheistic reverence.

From there, he would turn and gaze back at his house. At that distance, it appeared as little more than a tiny blue-white dot on the water's edge. Yet, it was his prize—a small bungalow resting comfortably on a hand-laid stone foundation, its weatherworn base hidden under a thick blanket of ivy and periwinkle.

Alan had waited several years for the property to come on the market. Then using his highly developed skill as a negotiator—the same skill that had allowed him to amass a small fortune and retire early from his job as an independent sales rep—he had paid cash.

Today, his anticipated view of the empty shoreline made the solitary pillar of rock especially inviting. Alan quickly climbed to the flat shelf near the top and leaned against the naturally supportive contour of the stone. Slowly, devoutly, he surveyed the entire beach—his beach. At least, that's what he told himself. And why not? He did, after all, have an innate appreciation for its serene beauty. And he was all too aware of how it suffered when subjected to the abuses of the ignorant and irresponsible—abuses he would never tolerate if the beach belonged to him.

Alan looked out over the water. "So, what will we discuss today? What secrets will you share with me?" The ocean settled his thoughts and he often talked to it like an old friend, his irrational personification of the sea a telling symptom of intentional self-exile. Since his retirement, he had deliberately distanced himself from personal acquaintances, colleagues, and former business associates, favoring his own company—and voice—to that of others.

Although he seldom had to wait for the waves to answer, today his confidante seemed restless and unsettled. Instead of welcoming him with the relaxing rhythm of a gentle surf, the water was agitated, churning with cross-currents and rip-tides. In the distance, burgeoning thunderheads were rising from the edge of the sea, and unlike the usual white blankets that spent the day playing hide-and-seek with the sky until finally resting on the sun-struck horizon like giant puffs of cotton candy, these intruders were different—threatening harbingers, an assault force from an angered Poseidon.

"Don't worry," he assured his anxious friend. "I'm sure they'll keep their distance."

His thoughts were well-intentioned, but in the scheme of the universe they were nothing more than idle chatter, and within minutes a dark rumbling umbrella extinguished the sun.

Bright flashes began to light the interior of the boiling cloudbank. In a threatening display of power, jagged razors of blue fire dropped from the sky, blistering the surface of the water.

"Shit. I probably won't make it back in time to beat the storm."

His bungalow was nearly a half-mile away, and as he hurriedly jogged along the shoreline, he regretted not being able to enjoy the pleasant, even roll of the surf, its normally soothing turquoise-trimmed waves now a chaotic frenzy of foaming white caps.

The wind arrived with the rain, the fierce gale driving the downpour sideways. As the drops stung his face he cursed his bad luck, slinging insults against the storm—and anyone else who might presume to ruin his day. "I'll give you a minute or two, that's all. Then you *will* move on, leave my beach."

As if mocking Alan's pretentious attempt to challenge its dominion, the tempest howled in defiance, stripping sea grape trees of their leaves and wrapping shredded fronds around the sodden trunks of swaying palms.

He looked around for the nearest shelter. There was only his familiar granite megalith some one hundred fifty yards behind him. Although it wouldn't keep him dry, he could sit out the deluge with his back against the stone, on the side opposite the wind and waves.

As he hunkered in close to the rock he felt the latent warmth of the sun, absorbed from an earlier cloudless sky. Irritated by the sheeting rain streaming down his cheeks, he formed finger tunnels around his eyes and peered through the curtain of water. He recognized the green blur of a plastic chair as it tumbled across the sand.

"Damn storm. It's crapping all over my beach. It's got to stop soon, before the trees snap."

If Alan had ever enjoyed the slightest preference from nature, this torrent confirmed his loss of favor. Unrelenting, the blowing wall of water strengthened in intensity, the whirling gusts clotting the air with saturated grit.

As the swells pushed the storm surge even higher, the huge projection of bedrock could no longer shield him from the reach of the sea. Wet and cold from the breakers that washed up high enough to touch him, he barely felt the bump of something solid against his leg. At first glance he thought it was a small Thermos. But as the receding surf moved it slightly outside his reach, he could see the cylinder-shaped object was covered with unusual markings—quite different from the bright patterns and bold graphics that typically decorated an insulated beverage bottle. He leaned into the wind, grabbing the oddity just before the rctrcating swells could return it to the ocean.

Even through the rain, Alan was impressed with his catch, the color alone making the object interesting enough to reward him for the reach. As the forces of nature jousted for dominance, Alan imagined how the piece would look on the front porch railing, or among his collection of shells lining the pea-gravel driveway next to his house.

A rogue updraft slapped his face with abrasive fury.

"How much longer is this going to last?"

The answer came quickly. Although he was grateful for the unexpected reprieve from the angry elements, the clouds swift retreat was as suspicious as it was welcome. Alan briefly wondered if his new souvenir was some kind of seafarer's talisman, granting its possessor the power to change foul weather into fair. The thought was a passing one, and in the time it took to jog back to his house, he had completely dismissed the rapid end of the storm as nothing more than a fortunate rebounding of atmospheric pressure pushing the exhausted thunderheads from the area.

After changing into dry clothes, Alan sat at his dining table to examine his new find. About eight inches high and three inches in diameter, it resembled a small lamp base. But there were no holes or seams from the process of manufacture, and the maker had left nothing that could be opened or twisted free to reveal the interior. One end had been finished with a smooth rounded crown while the opposite was flat, allowing the piece to stand upright.

The material from which it was constructed appeared to be a union of wood and stone, the combination so densely fused that it was difficult to determine which comprised the base component and which was inlaid. Smooth to the touch, the surface was patterned with intertwining ribbons of deep purple and burgundy, the colorful helix forming the unique design that had first caught Alan's attention as he pulled it from the water.

"It's just a bauble," Alan said aloud. "A rich person's trinket accidentally dropped from a passing yacht. Someone probably paid a small fortune for it, and now I bet they don't even know it's gone."

Alan glanced at his watch. There was still time to get his shopping done before the beach-plundering weekenders took all the good parking spots. He set the object aside, grabbed his grocery list, and headed out for the store.

A visit to the market usually took no more than an hour, but street maintenance on the main thoroughfare had strangled the traffic, stretching the round trip into a two-hour stop-and-go crawl. By the time Alan returned home he was fuming.

"Damn crazy tourists." Shifting his shopping bags from one arm to the other, he fumbled with his house keys. "This used to be a decent place to live. No traffic, plenty of parking, didn't have to fight your way down the aisles to get a loaf of bread. Now, it's overrun with—"

Alan stopped his ranting mid-sentence. His entire kitchen was bathed in rainbow–fused light. More curious than concerned, he tracked the brightly hued beams to their source—his newfound knick-knack. Picking it up, he felt a twinge of excitement as he watched the full spectrum of reflected sunlight dance in concert with the movement of his hand. "Must be some kind of prism," he said, his focus captured by the hypnotic display of color. "Good juju," he added, recalling how some of the Haitian street merchants referred to their good luck charms.

"I'll put it on the deck. That's where my juju bottle belongs."

He quickly changed his mind. *Someone will see it there and try to claim it.*

Although Alan didn't know exactly what his newfound treasure was or where it came from, he hadn't gone to all the trouble of retrieving it from the sea only to have some muscle-bound beach bum take it from him.

I'll keep it in the house, hang it from the main entry beam where it can catch the light for most of the day. Or on the windowsill, to reflect the late afternoon sun. I'll decide tomorrow.

Two

The Negotiation

The next morning brought a clear blue sky and a warm breeze—the kind of weather that always drew people to the seashore. He didn't want to think about it. Grabbing his light-bending novelty from the kitchen counter, Alan walked out the back door toward an old ramshackle storage shed. Providing minimal protection for a half-empty bag of potting soil and some replacement roof shingles, Alan also used it to store a few tools and some loose hardware.

He welcomed the opportunity to be outside, to be on the beach with purpose. Not to enjoy the tickle of the sun on his skin or to hear the soothing rhythm of the waves, but to revel in the sadistic pleasure of confrontation, to direct his pre-emptive arrogance at *them*, answering their questions before they could ask: *No, you can't use the bathroom. No, I don't have any water. No, you can't use the hose to wash off the salt. And no, I don't know what time it is.*

"Somewhere under the bottom shelf . . ." he mumbled.

Peering into the rusted-out coffee can, he stirred the collection of loose hardware— mostly nuts, washers, and bolts—with his fingers. "It can't be too big, might split the thing wide open." Finally locating a few finishing nails, he dropped them into his shirt pocket.

Brushing aside a thick blanket of cobwebs, he began rummaging through an old plastic paint bucket, pulling out a plunger, paint roller, and a broken hacksaw before finding the hammer.

The lack of a decent working area forced Alan to return to his kitchen. He sprawled on the floor. *I'll seat the nail an eighth of an inch or so before driving it deep with a full strike.*

Estimating the center of the cylinder's flat end, he marked it with a pencil, set the nail, and gave it a light tap.

Instead of penetrating, the nail bounced off the surface.

What the hell? Must be hardwood, maybe walnut or cherry.

He brought it up for a closer inspection. Although the nail-point had failed to scratch the finish, the impact had definitely affected its integrity. He could hear a soft hissing, as if the interior had been under pressure and was now equalizing with the ambient altitude.

"Probably been under water a long time. Got to let off some steam."

Re-positioning the nail, Alan swung the hammer again. This time the strike was solid, with plenty of force. The metallic ping of the nail ricocheting across the floor was suddenly lost to the sound of escaping air. Alan jumped to his feet, concerned the thing might explode or the rush of leaking gas might be filling the room with dangerous—even deadly—fumes.

"Maybe it's some kind of high-tech fire extinguisher or a CO2 dispenser for making wine spritzers." It was mere speculation and both possibilities were doubtful, especially since a puncture to either type of pressurized container would have sent the cylinder skittering across the floor.

With no reasonable explanation for its unusual behavior, Alan wanted it out of the house. Grabbing a broom he drew back, preparing to whack it—hockey style—through the open door. He focused on the target.

The sight made him lower his broom.

The object—at least part of it—was *moving.* As the inlaid bands receded into the base material, the once solid form was rapidly assuming the appearance of a worm-eaten section of turned wood, its metamorphosis leaving it riddled with deep channels and tiny chambers.

No longer able to hear the hissing release of air, Alan concluded that any danger from explosion had passed. He bent down for a better look. It reminded him of a child's puzzle, with interlocking pieces that could be removed to reveal a secret compartment. But this was clearly no toy. The obvious earmarks of intentional design reflected painstaking workmanship, the intricate symmetry more representative of fine sculpture than something mass-produced in the factories of Beijing.

Alan picked it up carefully and brought it close to one eye, peering into the elaborate maze of cavities and compartments.

"There is nothing inside." The voice was deep and sure and it came from behind.

Surprised, Alan twisted around on one foot, dropping the honeycombed remains of his juju bottle. It bounced off the floor and flipped up on one end, apparently able to right itself under its own power.

"There was, though not any longer," the intruder added. "What was once there is now here, standing before you."

Alan's first thought was that he'd caught one of the kids from the beach slipping into the house, probably trying to steal something. But this was no kid. And while he knew most of the local panhandlers, this guy didn't resemble any of them.

"What are you doing in my house?" Alan barked. "You can't just come in here and sneak up on me like that."

The stranger's mouth broadened into a wide smile. "Oh, I beg to differ. I can do exactly that. Actually, there is very little I cannot do."

His accent was dripping with a British lilt. Maybe Australian. His clothes—neatly-pressed khakis, a pale blue button-down shirt, and brown calfskin loafers—were yuppie-casual yet tailored to precisely fit his six-foot frame. His grooming was impeccable, with neatly trimmed sandy-blonde hair, a clean shave, and movie star teeth. Alan estimated the man to be about thirty-five.

"You need to get out of here before I call the cops. You hear me?"

"Why certainly I hear you. Although it's a wonder I can still hear anything with all that racket going on. I assumed I was being summoned to a situation of utmost urgency, so I came as quickly as the ether would allow."

"The what?"

"The ether."

Alan shrugged his shoulders, his rising irritation pushing him closer to picking up the phone and calling the sheriff.

"The ether seals," the intruder said. "The inscribed stonework that allows my coming and going. The helix is always in motion, sometimes offering the risk and reward of opportunity, other times simply foretelling an unchangeable future."

Alan knew that some of the "artistic" types occasionally wandered up from as far south as Key West, and a few of them could be eccentric as hell. He decided his best approach was to stay calm and try to get this guy out of his house before he could do any real damage.

"You're not from around here, are you?"

"Oh, contraire," the stranger answered. "I am from here . . . and there. In fact, I cannot think of a single place I haven't been. Places on and off this little sphere on which you live." He paused, his expression frozen in a flash of blank absence, as if in that fleeting instant he was somewhere else, distracted by another conversation. Then in a moment too short to measure, his attention returned, his features fully animated. "And I suppose you still call this part of your planet, oh, let me see, what was that word?" He pronounced it phonetically, in broken syllables. "Ah . . . mare . . . eee . . . ka."

"America," Alan repeated. "We say, America."

"Yes, yes, that's it!"

Alan nodded slightly in placation. "So what do you want?" It sounded demanding, and Alan immediately changed his tone, concerned the strange man might be harboring violent tendencies. "I mean, how can I help you?"

"I don't think you can. That is, I've never received help from anyone before. Never needed it. I appreciate the offer. Certainly do. I'm going to take note of it. Make sure you get full credit during the . . . negotiations."

Alan's eyes narrowed with building suspicion. The guy was talking in circles, but so far he hadn't given any indication he was dangerous, just a pain in the ass. He decided to try reasoning with him one more time before calling the authorities.

"Why don't you tell me why you're here? And what you want from me."

"From you? Why, I want nothing from you. At least not right away. Not until we get down to the finer points. And to answer your inquiry as to why I am here, I'm afraid I've been presumptuous, and for that I do apologize. For you see, I thought you knew. And here I've been going on about this and that, and you have no idea what's in store . . . for you." His last words lingered with unnatural duration, echoing through the house, each room answering in turn with a slightly smaller voice.

Alan wondered if the man was a ventriloquist or a magician working on a new act. He'd occasionally seen local street performers trying out new material on tourists, hoping to get feedback. *I'll compliment him on his talent—whatever it is—and then ask him to leave.*

Before he could say anything, the peculiar stranger continued. "First, it is proper and most appropriate that I introduce myself. My name is Efil."

Alan felt a tingle race down his arm and tickle the palm of his hand. A business card was tucked between his fingers.

It was probably there all along. Slipped it in when I wasn't paying attention. Some sleight of hand, that's all.

The card looked cheap—plain black printing on dull ivory stock. Yet as Alan squeezed the edges, it felt solid, as inflexible as steel, and so thin he could feel the pressure of his fingertips through the material. Across the top, four capital letters—EFIL—were prominently centered. Underneath, a single word: *Negotiations*. And at the very bottom, a string of unusual symbols:

EFIL

Negotiations

ɘnoʎɘ𝟣ɒIɘwɸɘ𝟣ilɛni

Unlike the complex and intricate depictions of pictorial cuneiform or ancient hieroglyphs, the strange characters appeared to be of a much simpler design. Alan briefly considered the possibility that the cryptic message was really a phone number or address written in an archaic language. Then he remembered an old business associate who got a kick out of disguising curse words in code, and he realized he might be looking at a camouflaged taunt that, when deciphered, would dismiss him straight to hell.

"E . . . what?" Alan thought it sounded more like a title than a name.

"Efil," he repeated. "Say it like this. Eeeeee . . . fillll. Now you try. Say it with me."

Alan mouthed the words, with little actual sound coming out.

The stranger seemed disappointed, but a moment later his huge smile flashed like the noonday sun. "Good! That's a start. And now, as to my purpose. More than a few have argued that I have none. Of course I take exception to my detractors, and assure you that my reasons for being here will be solely and completely determined . . . by you."

There it was again. This time the echo was intense, Efil's voice seeming to shake the very framework of the house.

"And now, having established the unlimited nature of my service," Efil continued, "I anxiously await your request. Have you any thoughts?"

"Is there someone you'd like me to call?" Alan asked. "Maybe someone who usually gives you medication?" Alan's initial frustration had turned into curiosity. And while he was still apprehensive about finding an intruder in his home, he no longer felt threatened. He was even deriving an odd sense of amusement from this eccentric's outlandish ramblings. He wondered—even wanted to hear—what the guy was going to say next.

"Perhaps I can offer a few suggestions," Efil said. "Let's begin with a review of the standard offerings. First, there is power. Always a winner, very popular. Next on the short list is money and all that it can buy. And then that old favorite—especially with the Greeks— love. Many of your historians believe the Greek concepts of love and life to be virtually inseparable. Frankly, it's my personal preference, but I don't push it as much as I used to, especially after that incident with Lot and his daughters, right after his wife became a saltlick for the camels. So there you have it—power, wealth, and love. Any of those sound appealing?"

The story was familiar, producing a flood of memories from Alan's childhood. *This guy wants me to think he's some kind of genie, like the one from Aladdin's lamp. He's obviously gone to a lot of effort with the scripted dialogue and the sleight of hand. And he's never broken character. Not once. Got to give him credit for that.*

Alan decided to play along and get the charade over with. The gag would surely end as soon as the would-be actor had granted him three wishes. "Okay, I get it. You're the genie and I'm the master—like in that story about Aladdin and the magic lamp. And now I have three wishes coming, right?"

Efil cocked his head to the side. "I'm not acquainted with this Aladdin fellow, but if it helps you to evaluate the possibilities of our new relationship, then by all means use it to your advantage. I encourage you to call upon all your memories, all your skills in our . . . *negotiations.*" Efil waited for the echo to stop, the sudden look of delight confirming his pleasure in listening to his own disembodied voice.

"I don't understand. You saying I got wishes or not?"

"You have one *negotiation.*" The word was still reverberating as he continued. "And with it, an outcome, a result. Perhaps even a consequence. If it makes it easier to consider our exchange as the fulfillment of a lifelong desire, then I encourage you to do so."

It wasn't the kind of rhetoric Alan had expected to hear. But if it would move this windbag out of his house without having to complete a police report, he'd go along with it—at least for a few minutes. "Okay, I got one wish coming. You ready?"

Efil's wide grin remained unchanged. "I am most certainly ready. However, you my friend, are not. We cannot begin until I am confident you are prepared to bargain in earnest—choosing your prize wisely, agreeing with the price, and approving the final terms of payment."

Alan could feel the prickly sensation of static electricity, the very air in his kitchen seeming to pulse with energy. Efil's body began to rise and in seconds he was hovering several inches off the floor.

"But it's my fault," Efil added. "Entirely my fault. Allow me to explain, to reveal the magnitude of the opportunity that awaits. For I sense great promise in you and with it, great purpose. You are, no doubt, truly gifted, a worthy negotiator with prodigious skills whose credentials surely include an impressive history of conquests."

Unable to divert his attention from the apparently-floating Efil, Alan reached behind, sweeping the air until his fingers found the top of an old spindle-back chair. Carefully lowering himself into the seat, he kept his eyes locked on the hovering spectacle. Although fascinated by Efil's implausible control over gravity—the effect even more spectacular as a strange blue glow began to surround and envelop Efil's body—Alan realized he had let his guard down. He didn't believe in the supernatural, and just because this genie-esque charlatan could pull off a trick or two didn't mean he should grant him automatic immunity from diligent and skeptical scrutiny. He had allowed Efil to distract, even intimidate him with a carnival stunt, a common ploy used to test the intelligence and perception of an adversary. Brushing his sudden—and rare—feelings of vulnerability aside, Alan retrenched, arming himself with reason and logic, the preferred weapons from his personal war-chest. While he didn't understand Efil's intentions, he would accept his challenge and engage him in the kind of confrontation in which Alan had always excelled—a battle of wits.

"There's probably a simple explanation for what you're doing," Alan began. "But I don't know what it is or why you're showing it to me. It's only a gimmick, a trick. I've seen so-called mystics and illusionists on TV do the same thing. If you really want me to believe you came out of that bottle and have the power to change my future, I'm going to need to see something a lot more convincing."

Efil displayed a calm and unaffected confidence. "Look outside."

"Why?"

"See for yourself. I thought it might help you to concentrate if I reduced the distractions."

Alan hesitated, feeling a little embarrassed that he had allowed this birthday party magician to bait him with the promise of proof. The very idea was ludicrous—asking Efil for irrefutable evidence to verify his identity as a supernatural being. Yet there was something about Efil's unflinching confidence, his self-assured presence . . . *and my God, the man was floating a foot off the floor!*

"All right, I'll take a look. Then you need to leave." Alan got up from the chair and walked to the kitchen window. "What I am looking for?"

"Everything!" Efil said. "Sometimes the details are hiding in the picture, and other times, the picture is hidden in the details. It's all there, right in front of you. Open your mind as well as your eyes."

Tired of Efil's cryptic banter, Alan began to turn away from the window, ready to insist that Efil leave immediately. At that very moment, Alan's mind finally recognized what his eyes had refused to see. Twenty yards from shore, the white curl of a small wave was frozen, the frothy water resembling a sculpted piece of glass. In the sky, several birds hung motionless in the air, their wings stopped in mid-flight. Eight feet away, a small pirate flag tied to the overhang of the deck was stretched full and horizontal to the ground without a breath of air to support it. Next to it, the tubes of a brass wind chime leaned at an angle, the striker in full impact—and not a tinkle broke the silence.

Bolting out the rear door, Alan ran across the deck and jumped onto the sand. Although afraid of what he would find, he had to see for himself.

Fifty yards away, a young couple had started to spread a picnic lunch. The scene resembled a distant snapshot—the blanket caught in mid-flap, the girl balanced on one leg, pulling off the shorts covering her bikini bottom.

Alan waited, half-expecting the couple to begin moving, not ready to believe the scene was anything other than a product of his own imagination—a kind of hypnosis brought on by subconscious suggestion. He blinked several times, as if Efil's likely influence could be cleared away like an irritating speck of dust. But the pair remained as still as the bubbles of glistening foam scattered like Christmas ornaments just beyond their feet.

Turning in the opposite direction, Alan spotted an old man surf-fishing in waders. Standing knee-deep in the arrested wake of a one-foot wave, he was hunched over in mid-cast, his body as stationary as a statue. Against the light blue sky, Alan could see the lead-weighted lure halted in route, the serpentine thread of green nylon suspended over the surface of the water.

The sea, the chimes, the birds, the people— the world—was quiet. Everything had succumbed to a paralytic silence.

Alan's instincts told him to run, as fast and far as he could, until he escaped Efil's reach. It wasn't safe to hang around with someone who could stop time. Even if it was only an illusion, this guy obviously had the power to manipulate the mind. In either case, Efil was dangerous. So why was Alan hesitating? Why wasn't he already high-tailing it down the beach?

He was deliberating. It was a process he used every time he faced an important decision—comparing the pros and cons, weighing risk against reward. He was sure Efil was selling *something*. And by continuing to listen, Alan could determine exactly what he was offering and at what cost. Then he could make an informed decision. An intelligent one. If the beach was Alan's church, logic was his god. And as his mind raced to find basis and foundation to rationalize the presence of this free-gifting, gravity-defying, effervescent demigod, a single thought overshadowed all others: *What do I have to lose?*

With slow cautious steps, Alan made his way from the sand to the deck and approached the open kitchen door. Inside, Efil was waiting, seemingly complacent—if not blissful—in the misty blue aura that surrounded him. Alan paused, unsure of how to tactfully interrupt a levitated life-form who was obviously parked in a zone of higher consciousness.

"I'm listening." Efil's voice seemed to come from everywhere.

"How did you do that? I didn't see your mouth move." Alan noticed Efil's eyes were closed. "Wait a minute. I didn't say anything. Can you read my thoughts?"

"I can," Efil admitted. "Or I can't. It is up to you. You were hesitant to approach, to advise me of your decision, so I took the liberty."

"Well, I don't like it. Not at all. I can't have you reading my mind. It gives you an unfair advantage. If this is really going to be a legitimate negotiation, my thoughts have to stay private."

Efil opened his eyes and broke into an easy grin. "It's done."

"How do I know you won't sneak a peek now and then—when it would be to your benefit to do so?"

"I will not lie to you. If I tell you that I will refrain from reading your mind, you can be certain that I will honor my commitment. Intentional misrepresentation will not serve my purpose. While I will always strive to make the transaction lucrative, I will not falsify my presentation or use deceit to accomplish it. I aim to strike a fair bargain, and assuring your satisfaction is one of my highest priorities."

Although Alan was far from ready to take Efil at his word, he was willing to set the issue aside for the moment. "So let me ask you this. Let's say I believe you, that I'm willing to go along with the idea that you have the power to grant me whatever I want. Now what?"

Efil's smile reflected total approval. "Yes! Now what, indeed! It is yours to decide. Your needs and wants shall serve us both. And I stand ready to begin."

"Okay, okay. I got it. The world is all sunshine and rainbows after you're done. Why don't you start by telling me how this works. Exactly."

"Ask for anything you like. Describe your request in as much detail as you can. You may include contingencies, conditions, or time limits. Fashion your dreams without constraint. Structure your future with abandon. Bring accidents of misfortune upon your enemies or sprinkle them with the rains of generosity. Blessings or curses—they are yours to bestow."

"And then you tell me what it's going to cost, right?" Alan's voice was dripping with caution.

"The cost is always commensurate with the value received. Especially when you consider the significance of what I have to offer."

Alan had kept the thought buried. Now he could no longer contain it. "It's my soul you want, that's the price, isn't it? That's the way these deals work, right? You give me anything I want in exchange for my soul."

Efil's eyes were electric, his pupils radiating staccato discharges of light. "On occasion I *have* bargained for souls, when the client's spiritual essence had evident and negotiable value. In your case, however, I will need to consider other assets."

Alan wasn't a religious man, but as a student of logic, he never bet against the unknown. If heaven *was* waiting, Efil's assurance that they would not be haggling over his soul—real or not—was a relief. "Okay, one more question. How long do I have before I give you my decision?"

"Oh, I'm afraid my offer expires upon presentation. You see, when I leave, so does the opportunity. And I must tell you, time grows short."

Alan had been enjoying his verbal jousting with the stranger, but now sudden panic set in. He knew the advantage of a deadline usually benefitted the one who set it. He had to think quickly, keep his mind on the prize. He was not about to lose his chance—if there was one—of striking a deal. Maybe the deal of a lifetime. "Okay, give me a few minutes. I need to think."

"Understandable." Efil nodded, the movement releasing a thousand tiny points of light that zipped back and forth inside the blue transparent cloud, the display clearly intended to remove any lingering doubt about his ethereal nature.

"You care if I think out loud?" Alan asked. "It might help."

"Not at all. In fact, if you desire I can assist you in sorting through things. Just provide me with the basics and I will compare the features and benefits, weighing the factors with impartial objectivity."

"But you won't trick me, right? I mean, you won't take one of my stray comments and make it my final decision, will you?"

"Of course not." Efil answered. "Upon the conclusion of our negotiations there will be no doubt in your mind—or in mine—concerning the exact nature of your request. I will take no action to bring your desire into fulfillment until you authorize it."

For most people, making such a choice would have been a daunting, even overwhelming challenge. But not for Alan. He had known from the start what he wanted. And while he could easily describe the end result, he wasn't exactly sure how to accomplish it.

Alan began to ramble, trying to organize his thoughts. "If I could close the beach, keep all the scum off . . . then I could keep it clean, let it heal. If I were somebody important, somebody with power, like the governor, I could pass a law making it private."

"So you're thinking about assuming the role of a politician, with the privileges and duties of the particular office?"

Alan thought for a moment. "You're saying if I choose to be somebody influential there would be responsibilities, other stuff to do that I wouldn't want to mess with?"

"If you take on the face, you wear all the expressions."

"So if I decided on a new profession, a position of authority, it's all or nothing? A package deal?"

"Exactly, a package deal."

"Look, what I want is to keep people off the—" Alan stopped. Being able to restrict others from his precious beach was only part of it. He also wanted to punish them for what they had done—for vandalizing the environment with their trash, disturbing the fragile ecology of the dunes, and forcing the wildlife to find a new, unthreatened habitat. Even more castigating than the penalty of exclusion, he wanted the guilty to experience the pain of absence. Like junkies deprived of their next fix, Alan wanted them to *need* the beach in the same way they needed air or food and water to survive. And most important, he wanted to relish in his retribution—*he wanted them to realize who was keeping them away*.

"I want to control this stretch of shoreline," Alan announced. "Keep others off. And I want them to know it's *me* who's doing it."

"Shall I place a high fence around it?"

"No, I want it open and inviting. I want them to smell the salt air and see how beautiful the water is, and then right before they can set foot on the sand, I want them stopped."

"How?" Efil asked. "How do you want them stopped?"

"I'll leave that up to you. You figure it out."

Efil shook his head. "Sorry, it's all about the specifics. Perhaps if we explore the different options and their consequences, you would be in a better position to—"

"You're making this complicated," Alan interrupted. "What if I make that part of my wish—for you to take care of the details after I give you the big picture?"

"If only I could accommodate you." Efil turned surprisingly serious. "But for a negotiation of this complexity, you'll have to provide me with precise instructions and the order of occurrence. Otherwise these things can, how do you say, blow up in your face."

"But you said you would help me work through the process." Alan's protest was charged with suspicion.

Efil shot Alan a reassuring wink. "Indeed I did. And if it's help you want, then it is help you shall receive." He paused, as if gathering his thoughts. "Let's examine your objective in its component parts. You want to keep others off the beach. Yes, yes, a good start." Efil's eyes rolled up until his pupils completely disappeared. Seconds later, they dropped back to their usual position. "Perhaps I could do away with it, eliminate it entirely, so no one could use it."

"No, you don't understand." Alan was becoming frustrated, not only with the increasing difficulty of trying to explain what he wanted, but also with Efil's nonchalant and seemingly procedural way of evaluating his request. "If you eliminate it, then I can't use it." Alan tempered his voice, extending his patience to uncommon extremes. "I still want the beach for myself. I just want to keep everyone else off."

"I see." Efil squinted, shooting a spray of electric glitter from the outside corners of his eyes. "You want to make it private. Exclusively for you."

"Yes! Now you've got it." Alan took a deep breath.

"Efil brought a hand to his chin, momentarily suspending his smile. "Hmmmm. Ownership is tricky. Lots of paperwork. Lots of records to change."

"So you're telling me you can't do it?"

"Didn't say that. I was merely reviewing the procedure, to make you aware of what's involved."

"I don't care what's involved. If I owned the beach I could prevent others from using it, right?"

"You certainly could."

"And they would know it's me who's keeping them away?"

"If that is what you desire. Perhaps you would like a large sign with your picture on it, so all would see who was—"

"A picture! I like that. A big sign with my picture on it." Alan easily visualized a fifty-foot-tall lighted billboard with *NO TRESPASSING* in big red letters across the top. And underneath his photograph, *By Order Of The Owner.*

"Anything else?" Efil asked.

"Punishment. There must be severe punishment for those who break my law."

"You mean subject them to a penalty or fine?"

"No. I want you to kill them."

Efil sighed. "I'm afraid that's not possible. Unfortunately, I can no longer end an individual life directly. I had to discontinue that option several hundred years ago. Things got out of hand. It created . . . imbalance."

"Wait a minute. You told me I could have anything I wanted. And now you're saying I can't do away with the bastards that trespass on my beach?"

"Oh, that's not the case at all," Efil assured him. "I can bestow you with weapons, superior strength, or the fighting skills of a warrior. I can grant you immunity from pain and make your body impenetrable to the attacks of your enemies. Then you may kill as often as you like, at your discretion. I just can't do it for you."

Alan fired back sarcastically. "Because it would throw things out of balance?"

"Yes, exactly. Out of balance." Efil's spirited grin returned. He was obviously pleased that his client understood this small yet apparently significant contingency.

Alan didn't like being baited with unlimited possibility, only to be disappointed with exceptions. "Are there other restrictions? Other things that are off-limits?"

"Nothing is really off-limits—for *you.* Your needs are best satisfied by your own actions. You wouldn't want me to make an error of interpretation because I mistakenly believed it would please you."

Alan's annoyance was growing and he pushed the point. "I'm not sure. I suppose it would depend on the circumstances, how big a screw-up I had to live with compared with the benefits of having everything taken of. For example, this 'out of balance' thing—are you talking about ice storms across the Sahara or the planet shifting closer to the sun?"

"Not exactly." Efil's expression turned thoughtful. "It's a bit more complex than that. Are you familiar with the inequities of temporal probability?"

Rather than admit an academic deficit—a weakness in the eyes of an opponent—Alan deflected the question with one of his own. "Like how?"

"Like Genghis Khan or Attila the Hun. You can't imagine the mess those two caused."

"Both of them were . . . clients?" Alan hesitated over the last word, suddenly uneasy with the knowledge that Efil's transactions had been conducted with some of the most notorious tyrants of history.

Efil's eyes turned backward as if retrieving the details of some nearly forgotten experience, and Alan wondered if Efil had the ability to peruse time, to watch past events through some sort of magical window located in the nether regions of his head.

"Hmmm . . . yes, here it is." Efil's steely pupils returned to their normal position. "They received full service. And with a guarantee of satisfaction," he added. "It cost a bit more, but they were willing to pay. More than willing. And I assure you, they received their money's worth."

"You offer a guarantee?"

"Why of course! It's my standard practice and an excellent feature, especially when you consider the damage that could result from unforeseen contingencies. In the past I offered it as an option. Now it's simply built into the price. And by making a small adjustment in terms—complete payment in advance—I'm able to provide the promise of satisfaction while eliminating the risk from unknown complications and liabilities."

The promise of satisfaction. Alan's grimace betrayed his efforts to conceal his immediate recognition of another variation on the old 'bait-and-switch' scheme. "Hold on," he began. "You never said anything about having to pay upfront. And now you're saying the results aren't guaranteed unless I pay a higher price? You can either deliver what I ask for or you can't. Dangling a guarantee in front of my nose as an incentive to get me to bite is just another scam. I'm not buying a used car here, so you need to back up and get your story straight."

Efil cocked his head to one side. "I assure you it was not my intent to misrepresent the terms of our arrangement. Being the skilled and shrewd businessman that you are, you undoubtedly understand it's sometimes best to reveal the specifics of a transaction a little at a time. So as not to overwhelm. I simply had not arrived at the point of full disclosure."

"Bullshit! You promised me one wish—"

Efil held up a single finger, effectively interrupting. "I promised you nothing. I have *offered* you one negotiation. And I have never used the word *wish*."

Alan tried to control his irritation. Revealing emotion was a sign of weakness. Staying focused—and persistent—was the only way to insure his ultimate success. "Okay, you said I could have one negotiation, and I'm holding you to it. Otherwise I'm going to ask for something you're not going to like. Say, for example, keeping you inside that bottle for a million years or so. Or maybe I'll decide to have you disappear forever."

As Alan huffed in self-congratulatory posturing, he noticed Efil's distinctive Cheshire smile had been replaced by an unmistakable mask of worry, his eyes struggling to maintain the neutrality of a vacant stare. Even more apparent was the change in his surrounding mist-bubble, the once-bright interior now contaminated with dark spinning eddies and twisting currents of gray. Efil's mouth began to move, yet there were no words, no sound of any kind. As his silent distress continued to escalate, Efil's face rippled and fluttered, oscillating between a blank gaze and contorted misery, the fluctuation so rapid as to be an unrecognizable amalgamation of half-forming, half-dissolved features.

Rather than succumbing to panic or fear, Alan found Efil's new instability humorous. "Hardly the look of someone who claims a heritage of advanced enlightenment," he scoffed.

Alan's words were still in transit when Efil's face suddenly stabilized, returning to its familiar rounded countenance. Unsure if Efil's quick re-composure was in response to his insult or if he had just witnessed the conclusion of a high-energy alien mind-fuck, Alan was barely able to contain his cocky delight in undermining the confidence of his opponent. "Have a good trip?" He made no attempt to disguise the sarcasm.

"Clearly I've underestimated you." Efil's broad smile was as self-assured as ever. "You're an excellent negotiator, well-versed in thc art of persuasion, truly talented in the ability to better a bargain."

Alan took it as hollow praise—an insincere compliment meant to gain influence over those less skilled, less experienced in the gambits of business. Even so, he nodded, knowing his response was expected.

Efil continued. "So this is what I'm prepared to do. I will waive the requirement for payment in advance, forestalling any personal sacrifice or indentured duty. Although these concessions will not affect the quality of my service, I will, of course, have to exclude the guarantee, making *you* completely responsible for the outcome you desire. How does that sound?"

"No payment?" Alan knew better. It sounded like another ploy, another attempt to double-talk him into something he would regret—and pay dearly for—later. "My wish has to have a price. Otherwise it won't have any value."

"Oh, I certainly didn't mean to infer I would fulfill your request without some kind of payment. I simply tailor the terms to suit your situation. And in this case, it will require your signature on that deed." Efil was pointing to the dining room table, where a legal-size document and pen had inexplicably materialized.

"A deed for what?"

"This house, this land, your part of the beach. It is the thing that holds the greatest value to you."

"I'm not signing over my home for some make-believe, pie-in-the-sky fantasy that may never come true."

Efil's mouth twisted into a forced frown, the way a circus clown contorts his expression to feign disappointment. "I thought we had established mutual trust, a bond between professionals, without misgivings or doubt. Yet you remain plagued with uncertainty." Efil's tone was laced with placating tolerance. "If you review the agreement, you will notice I have included a provision to delay the transfer of title until your demise. After that, why would you care?"

Alan wouldn't. In fact, he wouldn't give one iota about the place after he passed away.

Although he had a distant half-sister, he had no intention of leaving her such a valuable asset—especially after the confrontation he'd had with her holy-roller preacher-husband who'd tried to hold Sunday morning services on the sand directly behind Alan's house.

Still, the idea of payment on death troubled him. "Your terms would make my death a priority. The sooner I'm dead, the sooner you get my house."

"That is true."

"So what would keep you from re-arranging my future, causing me to trip and break my neck in the middle of the night? You could intentionally influence my health, give me some disease that would result in my premature passing and I wouldn't even know it."

"Ethical restraints prohibit me from taking such actions."

"I'll need more than that. I want some kind of assurance, in writing, specifically restricting your power over my lifespan."

"That's reasonable." Efil paused, as if formulating his next thought. "Your demise

51

will not occur prior to natural expiration unless you desire it."

"I would have to *want* to end my life early?"

"You would have to ask for it."

"You'll put that in writing?"

"I already have." The document rose slightly off the dining table, then settled to its original position.

Alan congratulated himself on another successful maneuver. He had secured the additional leverage he wanted, but he had to ask. "I'm curious why you're so flexible, why you're willing to wait until I die before you get your payment?"

"I do not regard time in the same way as you do. Whether your lifetime spans a hundred years or ends tomorrow, it's all the same to me. I only require that payment is agreed upon. Then at the proper time, I collect." Efil touched a fingertip to his chin, the movement leaving a wake of sparkling energy. "So, to review, I am offering the deferred acquisition of your property in exchange for no guarantee. Is that acceptable?"

Rescinding the guarantee made Alan uneasy. "Without a guarantee, what am I giving up?"

"Oh, the usual drivel contained in all contracts. The only real benefit you would relinquish is the right of cancellation—the right to return everything to its original state. But what would be the purpose in that? Clearly you are capable of managing your own affairs. Especially when you're certain the outcome will please you."

Efil's answer made sense. But could he believe it? Alan could easily interpret the most skillfully crafted doubletalk or recognize the subtle nuances of careful omission. He had honed his ability to interpret the tiniest vocal inflection, the most inconsequential body movement, by investing years of study—watching and analyzing people. But Efil was the first non-human negotiator he had ever faced. As he drew on his old and trusted principles of deduction and reason, he cautioned himself to avoid making the assumption that this uncorked gas-bag was going to behave in the same way as his terrestrial counterpart.

"I suppose I could refuse your offer," Alan began, "and decide to pass on the whole deal, let you go back to wherever you came from."

"Would that be your deepest desire—to leave your life unchanged?"

Efil's response surprised Alan. He had mistakenly believed that Efil *needed* to complete a transaction, much like a salesman with a quota to fill. Alan needed to regroup. "I feel like I'm being pushed into making a decision. I need a minute to think."

"Of course. Take your time. There's little to be gained in choosing hastily, especially if it later burdens you with regret."

Alan reviewed his situation. If he considered each aspect, every detail of the transaction, he could limit his liability, make sure there were no loose ends that might turn into problems. He was a smart guy. Even Efil had said so. And in this case, the praise was justified—his skill as a professional negotiator had allowed him to amass enough cash to retire twenty years earlier than his contemporaries. This was just another deal, another contest in which to use the aggressive bargaining protocols that had made him a wealthy man at an early age.

"Okay," Alan said. "I'm ready to move forward. And from now on, no more surprises."

"Absolutely."

Alan crossed his arms. "There's one final thing I need to make this arrangement work."

"Ah, the last objection, the concluding gambit in a well-played strategy." Efil was beaming. "Please, tell me. Let me fulfill your most anticipated desire."

"I want *you* to handle the initial and on-going termination of the people on the beach. I can't be concerned with personally eliminating those who won't obey my warning. I know you said you wouldn't do it, but that's the deal. Take it or leave it."

Efil's expression fell and for the first time, Alan was sure he saw a trace of genuine disappointment.

"*Take it or leave it*," Efil repeated. "You can't imagine how many times I've heard those words. And I've come to recognize the phrase as the mark of a tortured soul, someone who is as desperate as they are unforgiving. However, I believe you are cut from a finer cloth. Unlike those who ache for the blood of their enemy, you have countered my offer solely to procure the greater advantage. You pursue better terms if for no other reason than to make a good bargain even better. Your motives serve you well."

Although Alan discounted Efil's spill of philosophical rhetoric as monotonous prattle, he listened closely, hoping to discern elusive clues that would reveal his adversary's real intentions. But the rate of Efil's speech was unchanged from his normal cadence, and his tone and inflection conveyed nothing unusual. Neither did his eye movements or variations in micro-muscle fluctuations. From what he could determine, Efil was merely making an honest observation. And that was out of character—a suspicious break in Efil's consistent pattern of self-serving gratuitous behavior.

"Okay, Socrates, what's up?"

"Your request for early termination of third party lifespans requires a major deviation from my customary terms and conditions. I haven't made such an exception in hundreds of years. Not that I haven't been asked. Why I remember a rather polished gentlemen—not from around here, you wouldn't know him, he lived in a place called Landon or London, something like that—who begged me to deliver the mutilated bodies of harlots, tarts, and the odd strumpet to his doorstep. He demanded a new corpse every night, nice and warm, fresh from the streets. Well, you can imagine the difficulty, turning the act of random murder into a premeditated deed, the victim no longer his choice but mine. And me, having to trudge through those damp, foggy streets with knife in hand, searching for—"

"Okay, okay, I got it."

Efil's inimitable smile returned. "Excellent." The diameter of his blue bubble expanded several inches, the edges crackling with sparks and tiny electrical flashes. "It's a tribute to your intelligence that you understand my hesitation in even considering such a serious amendment to my customary offering."

"So does that mean the deal is off?"

Efil seemed to turn pensive, if that were possible, suggesting a moment of introspective deliberation. "I have often wondered what circumstance, what great adventure, what wondrous plan would motivate me to make such an exception. I had hoped such a concession would serve the greater good—a compromise for the betterment of humanity, a conciliation to benefit the majority. And while your desires may not directly reflect such lofty ideals, I see exceptional potential in you. You would be able to command great power yet have the opportunity to demonstrate responsibility and exercise restraint, particularly in ways that could ultimately affect you personally. The outcome could be... interesting."

What was he implying? Ethical imperatives and moral judgments had no place in this kind of negotiation.

Alan realized the measures were extreme, but he also knew his detractors would be the same low-life who believed the beach to be a convenient place to drain their car's motor oil, or the dunes the ideal location from which to covertly shoot the gulls with pellet rifles, then watch the poor birds slowly die in agony.

Alan was determined to protect his beach and if it resulted in a little collateral damage, then so be it.

"So what's your answer?" Alan glared at Efil. "Do we have a deal or not?"

"It's done." Efil nodded as he momentarily closed his eyes.

It was a common gesture used by salesmen to reassure a buyer before finalizing a sale, and it was what Alan had been waiting for. Now he was certain—Efil's attempt to sanitize the transaction with honorable intention was done merely to justify his concession, a ploy to salvage his dignity.

"Thank you." It was hollow, insincere. *But what the hell*, Alan thought. *I'll throw the poor bastard a bone.*

Confident that his business acumen and negotiating prowess was far superior to Efil's sophomoric skills, Alan turned his attention to the document resting on the dining table. A quick scan of the transfer deed produced the normal legalese. Alan picked up the pen, preparing to sign. He stopped before the ink could touch the paper. Efil's business card had suddenly re-appeared on the table, distracting him with its slow and constant rotation, its movement apparently unaffected by friction or gravity. "Are you trying to divert my concentration, keep me from reading something buried in the fine print?"

"Quite the opposite. I want you to examine every detail. Take the time to inspect every particle of information. I encourage you to inquire about anything that is unclear."

Efil's overly-pleased expression was a bit intimidating, but Alan dismissed it, deciding it was all part of the act. *Efil is trying to compensate for his poor performance, re-establish his credibility. I'll push him a bit, see how he responds to a conditioned objection.*

"I think I'll wait to sign this. I'll execute the deed after I'm sure you fully understand what I want and you've convinced me you can deliver to my exact specifications."

Efil tilted his head until it nearly touched his shoulder. "Certainly."

Alan noted Efil's movements, including the amount of time he maintained the awkward position. Right now, it didn't mean anything. If Efil did it again, in exactly the same way, it could signify he was in a similar, receptive mindset.

"Now, where were we?" Alan asked.

"I believe we were discussing the details of your desired outcome." Efil clasped his hands together, forming a steeple with his index fingers. "The specifics of which had something to do with reducing the number of people within the immediate vicinity."

"And the best way to accomplish it," Alan added. "That's when the deal started going south."

"It isn't necessary to re-visit those circumstances. I now have a much better idea of what you desire. Your goal is to prevent others from having access to this specific stretch of sand. Is that correct?"

"Right! I want them gone . . . all the damn people."

"All of them?" Efil asked.

Alan hesitated. If Efil was asking, it was probably for Efil's benefit. Alan commended himself for catching it. He would proceed with caution. "I'm not sure . . . about *all* of them."

"Then perhaps you want *less* people."

"Yeah, a lot less," Alan confirmed.

"Do you have a specific number in mind? If you give me the final count, I can distribute even allotments of gender and age over the entire beach, or deposit them at opposite ends of the strand if you like."

Alan walked to the kitchen window and stared at the still-paralyzed landscape. *If I hand-picked the crowd, I could keep the numbers to a comfortable minimum and surround myself with a better class of people. People who I might enjoy being around. People like . . . me.* "No, not a specific number. I want to choose who stays and who goes."

"And those who go, what shall be their fate?"

"I don't care what happens to them. I just want them gone. Permanently. Give them leprosy or turn them into shark bait. It makes no difference to me."

"Then you're leaving the means used to eliminate those whom you find undesirable up to me?"

"Is that a problem?"

"Not at all," Efil replied. "Simply a necessary disclosure, required when a client has relegated the power to inflict injury, illness, malady, or disease. So how shall we begin? Who will be the first to be purged?"

Alan spoke without hesitation. "The Asians. Start with them. Damn overachievers. They're likely to own this beach unless they're stopped."

"Done," Efil announced. "You're down nine percent."

"And the blacks. They leave the sand clean, but that god-awful crap they call music shakes my windows from three hundred feet away."

Efil gave him a reassuring glance. "They're gone. Anyone else?"

"Yeah, the Italians. They make great pizza, but they're the loudest goddamn people on the beach."

"Do you want to get rid of just the loud ones or all of them?"

Alan thought for a moment. How could he be sure a normally quiet Italian wouldn't suddenly feel the need to break the silence with a baying rendition of O Sole Mio?

"All of 'em," Alan snarled. "Take 'em all."

"Done. You have approximately 67 percent remaining. Is that it?"

"Let me think." Alan paused. "Well, there's the French. Nobody likes the French." Then he remembered the only two French people he had ever known—two women he'd met while walking the shoreline last year. Eventually they had wound up on his deck in the evenings, sharing a bottle of wine and chatting in passable English, unconcerned that their bare breasts might be socially inappropriate. Visiting for three weeks from their native Nice, they had managed to convince a few of the other women to discreetly shed their tops as well. "Wait! I've changed my mind. Leave the French alone."

"The French shall stay," Efil confirmed. "Who is next?"

"Hmmm." Alan had visited Germany several years ago, and he remembered the intimidating arrogance of the machine-gun-toting soldiers as they patrolled the airport. "Germans! Take those controlling bastards."

"By the way," Efil said offhandedly. "You're certain you don't have any German ancestors? If there is the slightest possibility, it's better to err on the conservative side."

"My people are from Scandinavia."

"Excellent!" Efil said, his happy demeanor suggesting he had satisfied another disclosure requirement of paranormal agency law. "Scratch the Germans. Keep the Scandinavians. Done."

Three

A Promise Fulfilled

The morning arrived on a soft breeze. Alan's first destination—even before the bathroom—was his rear deck. It offered the best view and with it, a count of early visitors. A large group—more than twenty within a hundred feet of his house—was a good indication there would be a crowd by noon. Less than ten usually meant lighter traffic, less scum to pollute the sand and water.

If Efil had made good on his promise, there would be no Asians, Italians, or blacks to be found. No Germans, Aussies, or Spaniards either. And that was only the beginning. It had been a long list, one that was eventually reduced to writing. It read like an inventory of the world's ethnicities and, after reviewing it several times, Alan had finally agreed. In exchange for removing the "undesirable masses" from a designated one mile stretch of beach that would now be under his exclusive stewardship, he had handed over the executed deed to his home.

As Alan stood on his deck, he surveyed the shoreline, amazed at the complete absence of people. Not another soul in sight. But it was early. He would wait an hour. Then he would walk to the far end, listening to accents, scanning faces. If necessary, he would introduce himself, waiting for a last name to give it away. And then he would know if that overstuffed turd of a genie had really pulled it off.

Coffee and a toaster waffle. With a little syrup. Then a hot shower.

Alan noticed it in the mirror as he was drying off—an area of discoloration, a rough patch of skin on the back of his neck. *A little aloe vera and it should be gone by tomorrow*. Pulling on a T-shirt and a pair of shorts, he headed outside.

67

He searched like a soldier hunting for land mines—cautious, almost certain he would discover what he didn't want to find. As he passed his revered stone outcropping, he was becoming hopeful—even giddy—at the prospect of having eliminated his tormentors. Although he had expected to find a handful of neutrals—day-tripping Frenchies or Swedes— he wasn't going to question his good fortune, especially since he could see a descending human horde subdividing the sand with blankets and umbrellas just beyond the north and south boundaries of his sanctified strand.

But here, on *his* beach, he walked alone.

He was ecstatic.

He spent the rest of the day on his deck, watching the sandpipers playing tag with the surf, feeling the sun bake his skin. Around mid-afternoon he fixed a light lunch and loaded a cooler with beer and ice to reduce the number of trips back to the refrigerator. As the shadows drew long across his deck, he felt a twinge of exquisite guilt. He was enjoying the beach like a privileged sovereign, euphoric in his solitude with only the birds, the breeze, and the sea to keep him company.

Four

The Final Cleansing

The next morning, Alan woke from a fitful sleep. His arms and legs hurt and he had a growing ache in his chest. "Some aspirin, that's all I need." He popped two in his mouth and closed the medicine cabinet, the swinging mirror catching a fleeting reflection of his back.

"What the hell?"

Repositioning the mirror, he noticed his lower left side appeared shrunken, making his torso uneven. He twisted at the waist, straining to see.

The sight brought a gasp of horror. A dark hollow stretched from his upper shoulder to the base of his spine. Weaving down his body like a snaking canyon, it was over an inch deep and equally wide. Alan traced the crevice with his fingers. "Oh my God! He's screwed something up."

Grabbing the edge of the vanity with both hands, he steadied himself, finally lowering his head to relieve a sudden onset of dizziness. "I'll pop the cork on that moronic shit-bag. This has to be his doing. I should have noticed it from the very beginning. No scarf, no purple sash, no turban. Definitely not old school. He's probably nothing more than a bumbling apprentice, practicing on unsuspecting victims until he completes some genie-trade-school internship."

Already wearing boxer shorts, Alan threw on a shirt and headed for the other end of the house. "I've gotta find that asshole and get him to fix this before it gets any worse."

All traces of Efil had vanished upon the conclusion of their negotiations—except for his bottle. Alan had found it yesterday on one of the end tables in the living room. Completely restored to its original shape, it looked the same as when he'd first pulled it from the ocean—except for the inset bands of deep purple and burgundy. Initially entwined in a spiraling helix, they now circled the cylinder as identical twins—separate mirror images with uniform spacing. Dismissing the significance—if any—Alan had left it on the table. Today he was supposed to return it to the waves at sunset. It was the final part of his agreement with Efil.

That conniving charlatan *had* to be inside.

Alan grabbed the bottle and began to shake it. "Hey! Get your ass out here. We gotta talk." Unconcerned about damaging his furniture, he began banging the container on the edge of the table.

A noise from the kitchen seized Alan's attention, arresting his hand mid-strike. It was an unmistakable sound—the closing suck of a refrigerator door as rubberized magnets mated with metal. In seconds he heard the snap and hiss of an aluminum pop-top. He turned and saw Efil standing in the doorway, holding a Bud Light in his hand.

The sight was ludicrous— a mystical genie, perhaps thousands of years old, helping himself to a cold one. It suspended Alan's anger long enough to make him realize he had to calm down. Confronting Efil with accusations of trickery or deceit would not be the best way to gain his cooperation. Alan would present his complaint with his usual guarded diplomacy—he knew Efil would probably expect a bit of verbal sparring.

"You drink *beer*?" Alan asked. "I can't imagine you drinking anything. Once you're sealed up in that little space, you're gonna wish you'd left the liquids alone. You could wind up drowning in your own piss."

Efil sported his typical tooth-filled smile, which by this time had become more than a little condescending. "Do you understand what the word *corporeal* means?"

"Uh, yeah. It means having a body, something like that."

"That's right! And while your concern is certainly appreciated, it's unnecessary. You see, once I return to my vessel I will no longer be of corporeal form. No bodily functions to worry about. I will wait as pure energy, ready to transform into physical form upon hearing the call from the next needy soul who is fortunate enough to—"

"Yeah, yeah, I got it," Alan interrupted, suspicious that Efil had already read his mind and was using rambling rhetoric as an intentional ploy to throw him off track. He quickly re-focused the conversation. "We need to talk."

"About?" Efil's sardonic grin grew even wider.

"About this." Alan lifted his shirt and turned, presenting his back to Efil. "What is this crap? You got anything to do with this?"

Efil flashed a look of contrived bewilderment, his expression no doubt refined by untold years of practice. "I thought it was what you wanted. To rid yourself of the . . . I believe you called them 'undesirables.' Yes, yes, that was it—*the undesirables.*" Efil's lips narrowed into an obvious congratulatory smirk.

"My wish had nothing to do with this." Alan pointed to his distorted torso. "There's a crevice here, a sunken trail that runs halfway down my body."

"Oh, that. I thought you were referring to the odd-shaped lesion on your neck."

"What?" Alan jerked off his shirt and reached for a hand mirror he kept in a drawer of the china cabinet. Bouncing his reflection off the silvered glass of an art-deco wall hanging, he examined the open sore. Approximately two inches in diameter, it was surely the offspring of the rash he had found yesterday. No longer superficial, the wound was surrounded by a matrix of deep splits, the irregular margin between malignant and healthy skin oozing drops of blood—an indication that the festering ulcer was devouring his flesh at a voracious rate.

Alan dropped the mirror. "Listen, you idiot, this is *me!* My skin, my body. Our deal was to get rid of the others, not mark me up with a set of bloody scales."

Efil set a pondering finger to his temple. "Let me see now . . . ah yes, I remember. You wanted certain people removed from *your* beach. You were very specific. During our negotiations I repeated your exact instructions for confirmation, so there would be no confusion, no mistake. You defined your enemy by common ancestry and bloodlines, demanding the elimination of unwelcome ethnicities and backgrounds."

Alan winced at his own words. "And so?"

"And so . . ." Efil repeated, his voice dripping with smug superiority, "that's exactly what's happening. Right down to every gene and chromosome."

As Alan began to comprehend what Efil was saying, he frantically tried to recall the offshoots of his family tree. He was sure of his own heritage—Scandinavian. His mother had told him. His entire family had emigrated from Sweden over a hundred and fifty years ago. "You're implying that I have a genetic connection to some of these . . . groups. I'm telling you that's impossible. You've made a mistake."

"That's very doubtful. Lots of due diligence goes into the fulfillment of every agreement, to avoid misunderstandings and prevent disappointments. But not to worry. I'll check on that right away."

Efil's face began to shimmer and in seconds, his head transformed into a sphere-shaped electrified blur.

Where the hell does he go? The metamorphosis no longer surprised Alan. In fact, he interpreted it as a sign that Efil was taking his complaint seriously. *He must have a set of files or some kind of computer—somewhere.*

The air around Efil's headless body crackled with streaking shards of fire, the display announcing his imminent return. His reanimation seemed to take longer than usual and for several seconds, Alan felt the eerie chill of his adversary's vacant stare, until Efil's eyes returned in a flash of iridescent blue.

"Yes, yes, it's just as I thought. Everything is in order. Everything correct. And by tomorrow you should be completely rid of all those negative influences. Of course, the lesion on your skin and the collapsing exterior is simply verification, an outward sign to confirm the process is working. Now, *inside* your body, ah, that's a different matter. Lots of cleansing and purging going on in there. Care to take a look?"

Efil was still the familiar showman, overtly inviting and synthetically friendly. And now, Alan saw something else—an air of control, of superiority, of having won. It was a professional negotiator's rare and singular privilege—to flaunt an intentional clue, hinting at victory after successfully maneuvering their opponent into a position of ultimate defeat. In a lifetime of deal-making, Alan had seen it only a few times, just before he had been blindsided with an unexpected and typically lethal move.

For the first time since meeting Efil, Alan was really scared. Efil's power was real, and it was having a devastating effect. The negotiation—his wish—was no longer important. Regardless of what it cost, he had to convince Efil to stop the damage and restore his health to its original state.

"Nothing to say?" Efil asked. "No words of appreciation? No heartfelt gratitude? Surely you can see the extent of my commitment, the quick call to action I have taken on your behalf."

"I never wanted my own body to be attacked."

"Oh? Just a moment. I have everything right here. Brought it with me, in case it became necessary to review the contract. You know how memory fails when disappointment rears its ugly head." Efil's eyes rolled, stopping in their backward position as if retrieving data from some ethereal hard drive. "Yes, yes, your instructions were precise, without ambiguity or interpretive license." His lids fluttered, like the wings of a butterfly flipping the pages of a large document. "Your directives are irrefutable and evidenced by your signature," he added, his eyes rotating forward to their normal position.

Alan made no effort to hide the thick swallow in his throat. "You're using our agreement to justify your own agenda, to harm me, change me. And I'm telling you I want it stopped." He felt something rake at his insides, a brush of cold needles sweeping through his constricted veins. He had to sit. He stumbled to the nearest chair.

Efil nodded, his demeanor one of total approval. "Ah yes, now you're beginning to feel it. It's so satisfying to see my best efforts coming to fruition. Undoubtedly one of the most gratifying rewards of my profession. It would warm my heart—if I had one."

Alan pressed gently on his abdomen, then flinched from the pain.

Efil continued. "So you can fully appreciate my efforts, let me give you an idea of what's happening to you. Your liver is down to half its normal size. Your lungs are shrinking, too. And your circulatory system will soon begin to contract—all that undesirable blood from your . . . wait, it's coming to me . . . an ancestor from twenty-two generations ago. Oh, yes! Things are coming along quite nicely."

"But I should be immune from the process," Alan argued. "It's not supposed to affect me. That wasn't part of the deal."

Efil fell serious. "You made no request for such immunity. '*All of 'em,*' you said. '*Take 'em all.*' You were very clear on that point. Even after identifying specific ethnic and ancestral exclusions, I gave you every opportunity to make additional exceptions to the purging. Perhaps if you had put a limit on how many previous generations were to be examined or when to stop evaluating genetic influence, you would be experiencing a very different result."

Alan glared at him with an equal mix of disgust and horror.

"You see," Efil continued, "your specie has many significant commonalities, not the least of which is original genealogy. I only had to go back a few hundred thousand years before I found a single genome, the unique helix, a master set of chromosomes."

"A few hundred thousand years?"

"Right! To the very beginning." If Efil's feet had been in contact with the floor he would have been dancing. "To put it into rather basic terms, all human-kind sprang from the same blueprint. Why, a mere jump of 30,000 years will reduce the number of genetic mutations and evolutionary adaptations to less than the number of fingers on my hand." Efil's fingers began to multiply in a blur of spreading digits. "Oh, I mean *your* hand," he added with a slight touch of contrived embarrassment.

"Frankly, I'm surprised you didn't think of it yourself. The fact that different physical characteristics and genetic mutations exist today is inconsequential—except to you. Call them what you will—German, Indian, Jew, black, or Asian—they are only variations on a common theme."

"But for the last hundred and fifty years," Alan protested, "my family has been isolated from the genetic influences you eliminated. That should count for something."

"One hundred fifty years. I'm always amazed at how you humans evaluate the significance of your own history. Do you have any idea how small a period of time that is?"

"Pretty fuckin' small?" Alan had lost control of the conversation and was employing his usual tactic of distraction by injecting a bit of humor. This time it didn't sound funny.

"That doesn't even come close," Efil countered. "It's *infinitesimally* small. Especially when compared to the total number of years your planet has existed. But as I explained, time is not the issue. It all goes back to your originating genetic material, with its unique and fundamental design including every alternative, distinction, and disparity. What you see as aberrant mutations—skin color, the shape of a brow or eye—is the result of *recombination*, a physical display of seemingly limitless permutations. And yet despite the peculiarities and deviations, the unmistakable imprint—the genesis—of humanity is always there, always present, confirming common origin and ancestry." Efil paused, his expression turning thoughtful. "It is a most curious singularity, and I suppose in a truly fundamental way, it actually makes the human race . . . *a family.*"

"So stop it! Put it back the way it was. Bring everybody back. They can have the beach!"

"Oh, my," Efil said. "I'm afraid that's a no-can-do. A bargain was struck. And you agreed that a guarantee was unnecessary. There's really no way to change the result."

"Of course there is," Alan argued. "You started it. You can stop it. Just reverse the process. I'll give you anything you want."

Efil lifted his chin. "It doesn't work that way." He hesitated, as if needing to simplify his explanation with condescending clarity. "Perhaps this will help you understand. Unlike less temporal beings, your life has a specific beginning and end. It cannot be repeated."

Alan slumped in his chair, his face drawn. "So what?" he managed.

"Don't you see? It's those very constraints that define its direction—*always forward*. Although it may sound like an observation of childish simplicity, I assure you it is a profound fact. Your life cannot be lived backward. If an outside force attempts to change its course—reverse it—your life would stop. I believe you refer to such an event as an *untimely* death." Efil waited for a few seconds. "Does this make sense so far?"

Alan hung his head. "Nothing makes sense. I just want to stop this despicable process from eating me alive."

"Which brings us to the unpleasant truth," Efil chided. "So listen carefully, because I'm certain you'll find this part especially interesting. My transactions, when accompanied by a guarantee, are delivered in two parts. The first is a fantasy—no less real to the client—but an illusion nonetheless. If you had requested a guarantee, you would have received your desired outcome in the form of a temporary, but voidable alternative existence, separate from the on-going timeline. Think of it as a kind of rehearsal, a test run. Of course from your perspective it would have been absolutely real, progressing until enough events had transpired for you to evaluate the result. Then, when you were certain it was exactly what you wanted, I would have made it a permanent part of reality."

Alan threw his hands in the air. "So wave your magic wand or spin your eyes around three times and fix this. Hell, if it's easier, make it temporary and then change things back to the way they were."

Efil offered the unmistakable look of pity. "*Change things back to the way they were*," he repeated softly. "Sadly, an all-too-frequent request. Of all the idiosyncrasies of your species, it is the one I find most fascinating—the failure to recognize the fortunate nature of one's circumstances until realized from the bitter regret of hindsight."

"Dammit, Efil, give it to me straight. What's the bottom line?"

Efil's eyes began to darken from the bottom up, filling with an inky fluid. "There is no going back. While my powers allow me to bend time, I cannot reverse it. If you had secured the guarantee, you would now have the option of accepting the results or rejecting them. However, in your insistence to bargain for better terms, I was obligated to deliver your outcome in real time. And therefore, what you see happening, what you are experiencing, simply and quite permanently . . . *is*.

Five

A Dream Come True

Alan had been afraid to go to bed, worried that he would wake up far less a man than he'd been the day before. But sleep came easily, and so did the dreams—visions of his body twisting and contorting, each spasm a prelude to ejecting a fist-sized knot of skin and bone that systematically diminished his form in a continuous and mutilating discharge of small bloody lumps of tissue.

The delusory scenes were graphic and disturbing. Yet Alan retained an uncanny awareness and perspective that allowed him to remain detached from the horror, his fragmented recollections reminding him that he had wished for—and received—*something.* And while the specific details eluded him, he knew it was something he regretted. Now his mind was being subjected to purgatorial review, perhaps a prerequisite to being given the opportunity to ask God for forgiveness—he hoped.

Using his protective logic like a shield, he held it close, tempering his fear as each chunk of flesh hit the floor, sprouted tiny legs, and ran from the room. Curious about their destination, he found he could change his vantage point by merely willing it. Floating up and out of his body, he moved through the ceiling, into the attic, and onto the rooftop, where he watched pieces of his former self race from his house like headless, bloody rats. Once on the beach, they skittered along the water's edge until eventually nestling into permanent residence among the countless grains of sand.

It went on for hours, the expelled parts dropping away, followed by the germination of legs, and then a swift pilgrimage to the beach. His beach. His parts. And they were quickly becoming one.

Constant self-reminders that it was only a dream helped to galvanize his emotions. Disturbing? Yes. But of real concern? Not hardly. After all, he would soon wake up and return to his sun-drenched shoreline, one that would welcome him with gently lapping waves, a cool breeze, and at the far end, a waiting throne of dark granite—the perfect spot from which to survey his kingdom.

Only once did he question his logic-based immunity, when a particularly large section of quivering tissue separated from his trunk—his ears filling with the ripping shred of tendons and muscle, the wet, sucking sound announcing its impact with the floor. Out of necessity and scale, the legs that grew from the rejected mass were commensurately larger. Even so, they strained against the weight, the load made more cumbersome by a core of dangling vessels that left a wide trail of thick, clotted blood.

From the beginning he had wanted to wake up, to end the dream. This too, became part of his nightmare. And as his ethereal essence continued to observe the grisly images of his own deconstruction, he realized that distinguishing perverse fantasy from trusted reality was becoming increasingly difficult.

With what little control he could muster, Alan forced his mind to consider one final thread of logic: *If I were awake, would I know it? How would I tell the difference? Am I awake now?*

Before the morning came, before first light could saturate the ocean with color and infuse the sand with warmth, Alan was gone. However, unlike a body suffering a traditional demise, his physical remains comprehended an awareness of his environment—a sensation of the elements, the rough grains of silica and quartz, the grit of shell and coral—always touching, always near, especially when an abrupt and temporary pressure brought them even closer. It was as if someone was walking the shoreline, compressing the sand against the scattered collection of his parts.

Granted the dubious gift of disembodied consciousness by the beach, by God, or as a parting gift from Efil, Alan's eyes—or what was left of them—still recognized his surroundings, although the details were hazy and indistinct. He questioned why he deserved such privilege, then immediately admonished himself for trying to understand the intentions of a much greater intellect. Instead he decided to focus on the miraculous nature of his fragile—and undoubtedly temporary—existence, before his body surely succumbed to the absolute powers of decay and decomposition.

With his perception reduced to a small circle of blue sky, Alan felt a sense of satisfaction, even joy as he recognized a passing filament of white. He wondered if it was the stray edge of a cloud or a fishing pole in close proximity, bending under the strain of a sudden strike. The wash of a wave blurred the picture and, without eyelids, it took nearly a minute for the salt to clear from the cells that had once comprised his pupils. By Alan's measure it was an uncertain eternity, and he looked forward to the return of his vision the way a schoolboy waits to welcome the Saturday sun. But as distinctions of shape and hue emerged through the brackish glaze, he knew something was wrong. His window of turquoise sky was now a bloody panorama of shadow and harsh silhouette. With his remaining moments too precious to measure, Alan could only assume he was facing the final shroud of death—a red veil announcing his arrival at the mouth of hell. But if this was a specter from the hereafter, why were there letters from the alphabet, spread large and bold across the canvas of tainted light?

Alan's recognition of the truth inspired the instinctual need to pull air deep into his nonexistent lungs, to *feel* the sense of respite that he would have previously enjoyed as a wave of relief. What he initially feared to be a threatening preview of purgatory was simply a discarded candy wrapper backlit by the sun, the red paper fogging his vision with a scarlet pall.

Motivated by curiosity, perhaps even driven by desperation, Alan concentrated on the letters: T ... O ... O ... T ... S ... I ... E

Lingering threads of memory filled in the missing words, completing the brand name: *Tootsie Roll Pop*. He was about to congratulate himself on stretching his powers of reason and cognition when the shock of his situation suppressed any desire to indulge in self-accolades.

This could be the final image I take with me into eternity—a piece of trash. Unless someone sees it . . . unless someone picks it up.

As if summoned by his weak yet still lucid thoughts, the wind lifted the wrapper into the air and sent it flying down the beach.

Another wave rushed to the shore. This time, heavy back-currents limited its rise. And while the water had mercifully spared his vision from briny contamination, the sea had left something in its retreating wake, depositing it directly in front of his dwindling acuity.

It wasn't paper—he was sure of that. It lacked the expected consistency of wet cellulose.

Shifting cloud shadow kept Alan's residual consciousness guessing. The object was familiar—his memory stirred more by what was missing than what remained. Like the crumbling framework of a long-abandoned house or the scattered debris left in the aftermath of a hurricane, it seemed incomplete, damaged.

Compensating for his diminished faculties, Alan began to discriminate between shade and silhouette, discerning the difference between solid and shadow. Although it took several minutes, his new virtual senses finally allowed him to recognize the object.

Efil's bottle.

Perhaps it had drawn its energy directly from Efil and with his departure, it could no longer maintain its form in an alien world. Or maybe the container had exhausted its power for self-preservation. Regardless of the reason, it was at the obvious end of its life.

Even with its former integrity reduced to a skeletal shell, the design of some netherworld artisan was clearly visible. The bottom of the ruptured frame contained a matrix of mirrored squares, each tiny reflecting plane revealing the internal surfaces in the same way a kaleidoscope displays prismatic multiples of a single subject.

Alan thought of laughing, but didn't know why—or how.

As the rising sun illuminated the very deepest part of the violated remains, the retreating shadows exposed more evidence of meticulous workmanship. Seamless joints and the flawless mating of a thousand miniature components belied Alan's original assessment of the object as a bauble or trinket.

A glint of light drew Alan's attention to a section of the interior conspicuously absent of the complex technology, a space seemingly dedicated for the small rectangular plate— surely gold or its alien equivalent—embedded into the sidewall. Alan's first assumption was the most obvious—it was the maker's label, the single line of symbols etched into the bright metal identifying the place and time of construction.

But why did they strike him as familiar? Had he seen them before? He remembered taking his first look at the container's interior after Efil had left the vessel in an invisible swirl of hissing gas. At the time, the minuscule row of characters could have easily escaped his percipient mind, his racing intellect dismissing them as a series of scratches or a manufacturing defect.

That sentient part of Alan that lingered was beginning to fade, his virtual senses diminishing. And yet he refused to give in to the darkness. With his limited perception begging for clarity, he focused on the strange rune-like figures.

It came as a flash of insight, bursting through Alan's impaired consciousness the way a bolt of lightning cuts through a clouded sky.

Efil's business card!

When he'd first held it between his fingers, the card's nonsensical cryptogram had seemed unimportant, perhaps declaring Efil's credo in some extraterrestrial language—or possibly just a crude joke. Now as the multi-mirrored matrix reflected the line of text, Alan saw the ultimate clue Efil had willingly disclosed, the essence of what he had failed to learn, and it brought a flash of bitter recognition.

Finally, Alan understood. He had been granted these few extra minutes of disembodied awareness to receive a prophetic and final revelation—to understand the reasons for his demise, to make sense of the insanity that had reduced his body to permanent obscurity on a Florida beach.

Efil's arrival in Alan's life had not been without motive or purpose. From the moment Efil first appeared in his kitchen, Alan had continued to speculate about Efil's true identity, hoping it would be a clue to his intentions. Vacillating between conjecture and assumption, between the possibility of an ageless genie with magical powers or a galaxy-hopping alien wielding advanced technology, Alan had finally dismissed the question, preferring to concentrate on the potential gain to be derived from the relationship rather than dwell on Efil's background and origin.

It had been his first mistake.

No doubt on some distance world—or in an alternative dimension—Efil's power was as common and natural as the presence of Alan's five mortal senses. But from a human perspective, Efil was a life-form that defied description, his abilities unexplainable, at least by any language on earth. That fact alone should have cautioned Alan to learn more, to find out in the most specific terms possible, *who* Efil really was.

Now—and much too late—Alan realized that Efil's guise as a purveyor of opportunity had been a ruse of overwhelming proportion. Whether sent by God, a mother race, or an ever-vigilant overseer responsible for maintaining collective balance in a chaotic universe, Efil's "negotiation" had been a carefully orchestrated tribunal—a final chance for Alan to redeem himself, to prove he was worthy to draw his next breath, deserving to take another step among those whom he so strongly despised.

Efil had been a messenger, a facilitator of fate, sent to evaluate Alan's birthright. But in Alan's haste to manipulate the circumstances, to exploit others for his own selfish ends, he had failed to recognize that the final prize under negotiation was not his seclusion, but his very existence.

In that very instant before Alan's senses were extinguished forever, the sun's rays struck the small golden plate in Efil's bottle, illuminating the single line of previously indecipherable script. Reflected by the surrounding manifold of unearthly glass, the string of symbols branded the sand in a mosaic of iridescent rainbows. And there, cast in silhouette by each chromatic arc, were the five words that had sealed Alan's fate—words that now served as both eulogy and gravestone:

In Life We Are One

Notes From the Author

I wrote *The Beach* as an allegory, denouncing those monsters who have dared to think themselves worthy of using extermination and terror in an attempt to recreate the world in their image. While the inspiration for the story is drawn from the darkest pages of history, the source of certain physical elements, especially the large granite outcropping from which Alan often surveyed his never-realized kingdom, was derived from a much more personal experience . . .

Several years ago I was visiting a Jewish synagogue to attend the marriage ceremony of a long-time friend. I arrived early and since I'd never been there before, I took some time to enjoy the beauty of the grounds and the extensive gardens.

I first saw the five-foot-high granite obelisk from a distance. It was in a curious location—at the intersection of two sidewalks. Yet with its geometric shape and sheer size, it invited as much attention from its simplistic beauty as it did from its placement. As I approached the stone I noticed it was engraved on a single side, requiring visitors to face east to read the inscription.

Instead of the expected Temple dedication or words of appreciation to a generous benefactor, it was simply a list—places and names that I didn't immediately recognize: Bogdanovka, Janowska, Majdanek, Ravensbruck, and Sobibor. But as I continued to read, others were horrifyingly familiar: Dachau, Chelmno, Belzec, and Auschwitz.

At the bottom of the list, two words stretched across the granite:

"NEVER FORGET"

It was a reminder. A warning. And a damn good one.

Clues, codes and Efil's bottle . . .

The construction of Efil's bottle was both a flight of fantasy and the result of a little research into the field of optics and light. No doubt some readers quickly deciphered the message printed on the bottom of Efil's business card because of the way the brain can automatically reverse perspective and order. It's similar to the process that allows us to recognize the image of an old woman and a beautiful young girl in the classic and often reprinted example of perceptual illusion. I'm also sure there were a few of you who took the line of text to a mirror to view the reflected page.

If you would like to see a real-life example of this projected reverse image phenomenon— much as Alan did when he saw the inscribed line of text from Efil's bottle cast upon the sand—take a look at the passenger side mirror on any late model car. Etched into the mirrored glass are the words: *Objects in mirror are closer than they appear.* When the sun strikes the glass at the correct angle, those words will be projected in reverse onto the car door.

In an attempt to make the clue on Efil's business card a bit more arcane, I used the equivalent Greek letters of Efil's name—which I'm sure most of you recognized as the word "Life" spelled backward—to separate the reversed words. In cryptology these are called *nulls*, and are automatically removed or ignored by the recipient because of their inherent familiarity or personal significance (or by the use of a precut mask or digital filter). Efil inferred this possibility when he began to explain the wide range of options available to Alan: "*And then that old favorite—especially with the Greeks—love. Many of your historians believe the Greek concept of love and life to be virtually interchangeable. And frankly, it's my personal preference . . .*"

While this may seem to be a very obscure inference, a formally trained professional negotiator—as Alan professed to be—is always listening for the interpretive and alternative meaning of every conversation. And from what I learned about the profession, Efil's subtle suggestion would have been recognized as a *significant revelation,* especially by those who use these specialized communication skills at the highest levels of proficiency.

Alan's skill as a negotiator . . .

Although Alan is fictitious, the skill attributed to his character—the ability to decipher an individual's intentions by acute observation—is not. If you're interested in learning more about this fascinating topic, there is a wealth of information available from books, training courses, and seminars. The discipline is called Neuro-linguistic Programming, or NLP for short. Books and home study programs will provide an introduction, however, proficiency is usually acquired through months of classroom-based instruction or personal tutoring. While researching the topic for this story, I was invited to attend several classes and workshops. I found even the limited amount of training I received incredibly useful, especially after I discovered how much of our communication takes place beyond the limitations of language and vocabulary.

References to stereotypes and cultural presuppositions . . .

When Alan was given the opportunity to determine which groups and ethnicities would be removed from "his" beach, his natural inclination would have been to choose specific ethnic groups and then associate them with the destructive activities he was so adamantly trying to prevent. For example, "the such-and-such race leaves their half-eaten hot dogs all over the beach," or "the so-and-so people toss their empty beer cans into the surf." And while I knew Alan would not hesitate to make such prejudicial accusations, I did not want one of my protagonists adding new negative stereotypes to the collection of racial, ethnic, and cultural presuppositions all too often propagated by the media and entertainment industry. So when it was time for Alan to demonstrate his shallow and self-centered importance by explaining his rationale for choosing which groups to be purged, I decided to restrict his reasons to existing and widely held clichés, hoping these less offensive—but certainly not more accurate—typecasts would be sufficient to reveal Alan's character.

The story's location and setting . . .

Contrary to the popular notion that Florida beaches are blessed with constant sunshine and warm weather, there are some parts of the state that experience seasonal changes in both temperature and rainfall. This is especially true in the northern panhandle of the state, where winter temperatures ranging in the forties and fifties easily create the deserted beach setting that was so appealing to Alan.

A Prelude to *Short Time* . . .

I'll leave you with a brief note of preparation for the next story. When considering a logical and appropriate companion to *The Beach*, my novella *Short Time* was an easy and obvious choice. Without revealing any details, there are some underlying and thematic similarities that made these two stories a perfect pair.

Short Time is best suited for the adult reader. It contains mature language and the story opens with an adult situation. Without apology, I encourage you to wrap your mind around this raw psychological narrative of exploitation, subjective truth, and brutal consequences.

Choices are made in brief seconds, and paid for in the time that remains . . .

Paolo Giordano

Short Time

ONE

Living On Credit

"Slow down, take it easy. You're acting like this is going to be your last piece of ass."

I relaxed my grip and lifted my hands, leaving red dimpled imprints where I'd squeezed her thighs. *Marking her.*

"I'm small, like a pixie," she'd said on the phone. "And I'm expensive. VERY expensive."

"You worth it?" I'd asked.

"You won't have any complaints."

She was right—worth every penny.

She was a tiny girl, perfectly proportioned with gravity-immune breasts, a sculpted waist, and Pilates-toned thighs. Her entire body was brown from the sun, the color unbroken by tan lines, and when she'd first laid back on the bed, I'd been content to run my hands up and down the entire length of her, letting my fingers linger in the cracks and crevices, amazed by the smoothness of her skin.

Her face had a comforting welcome, not pretty the way a high school homecoming queen is pretty, but still softy innocent, without a hint of the hardness that was no doubt building just under the surface. I especially liked her short dark hair, and the way she let me grab it from behind as I play-forced her head down on my cock.

I wondered how old she was, and then realized I didn't care. I leaned back against the headboard, deriving nearly as much pleasure from watching the muscles in her butt flex and quiver as I did from the skill of her mouth.

"You didn't pay for all night so we need to wrap it up." She looked up at me with a childlike seriousness that reminded me of my neighbor's daughter asking me to buy another box of trail scout cookies.

"How much for all night?"

"Another five thousand."

"You're not worth another five thousand. No whore is worth that kind of money."

"Then it's now or never, stud. I can give you another ten minutes, that's all. So you better climb on if you want to finish."

I tucked her slight form underneath me and slid inside.

Tomorrow I'll have myself a couple of blondes. But no dye jobs.

Two real blondes.

TWO

The Reckoning

I'd almost convinced myself they wouldn't come for me. I suppose I was hoping they would change their minds or decide I wasn't worth the effort of retrieval.

But they did come, waiting for me outside my house, shooting me with a tranq-gun before I had time to realize who they were.

"It's past midnight," I'd heard one of them say before they dropped me to the floor. I have no idea how long I laid there, drifting in and out of consciousness, before finally feeling the pinching pain of compression straps on my arms and legs. I opened my eyes to a disorienting blur of harsh florescent light spilling into unfamiliar hallways punctuated by flat gray doors and the distorted expressions of strangers.

I was moving, restrained to a gurney.

I struggled to make sense of it, to understand the rush of activity around me. But lingering in a barbiturate daze, my perception was as numb as my arms and legs.

I remember tape measures stretched over my body. And cameras—some with flash, some without—within inches of my face. There were questions, not directed at me, but about me. I'm sure I tried to answer, my spill of incoherent mumbles explaining the frequent order to shut up.

They were still poking and prodding just before someone threw a sheet over me. The sensory shock brought a fleeting moment of clarity, and I wondered if it was meant to prevent me from seeing something that might reveal my location. Now I realized it was done to reduce movement anxiety, the same way a dog or cat's cage is covered to keep the animal calm during travel.

*   *   *   *

The lights were on. That was different—I could swear the room had been dark when they wheeled me in. I wasn't on the gurney, either. I was lying on my side, suddenly aware of the unforgiving inflexibility of concrete.

I fought to focus, trying to establish a timeline. Had I been brought here by plane? Was I in the States? I had no idea how far I'd traveled. Somehow I'd ended up here, in this tiny, stark room. Wherever *here* was.

Disoriented, I wrestled with shadowy specters, fragments of phantom images, sometimes just strings of words without start or finish playing over and over in my head. In spite of my muddled concentration, my enemy wasn't confusion. It was the Ketamine, pushed into my bloodstream at close range by a Dan-Inject rifle.

I could sense there was more—events and conversations begging to be connected. I would have to wait, allowing my brain to reboot in segments, the way a dark city begins to relight after a power failure.

Even with my limited cognition, I was reasonably certain this vacant reach of concrete—approximately ten-foot square—was not a confinement cell in some state prison or a holding tank in a city lockdown. Its last remodel had left too many clues—the sprayed acoustic ceiling, the short base molding on the walls, and underneath, a gap where the floor covering had once met the sheetrock. Farthest from the door, a shallow alcove encouraged personal hygiene with a metal toilet and sink. The partition next to the commode held the recessed interior of an old medicine cabinet. The mirrored door and shelving were gone.

I listened for a familiar sound—a TV or radio, a running shower. But if there were others occupying the rooms next to me, they exhibited no routine, no actions borne from habit or discipline. Even last night, in my semi-conscious state, the only noises I remembered hearing came loud and forced—uneven footfalls broken by a flurry of activity, followed by a series of slamming doors.

And then, stone quiet.

Like now.

A shaft of dingy yellow light pushed its way through a single fixed window, piercing the room with a sallow column of choking float, the tiny fragments of dust riding nervously on the stale air.

I tested my muscles. Some of my fingers still lacked feeling. My right hip and shoulder ached, probably from when I'd fallen or been dropped. I had to get to my feet, to take a look outside. With more of a stagger than a walk, I made it to the window and held on to the chin-high sill, straining to keep my balance.

Eighteen inches square, the glass was internally reinforced with a cross-hatch embedment of quarter-inch steel rod. Unlike the captives it restrained, it was unbreakable.

Although an external security cage restricted my view to twenty feet in either direction, I could see enough to confirm that the narrow brick alley contained nothing but trash and graffiti—no signs or addresses that might give me some idea of the neighborhood, or for that matter the city.

I should have known better. These people were thorough, exhaustive. They had methodically removed all geographic information, systematically neutralizing all clues to the building's location.

I could only guess my room was part of a larger complex—probably a hotel or apartment building converted into a secure safe house, now on permanent lease from some off-the-books division of the state department.

I stumbled across the room and laid my shoulder against the metal security door. It was like trying to push through a block wall. I attempted to open the center access panel, a small sliding hatch used to deliver food. But the construction was the real deal—rivets instead of screws, heavy steel plate rather than thin gauge alloy or composite. Even the built-in projecting shelf was braced to the point that it easily supported my entire weight.

Suddenly lightheaded, I turned my back to the door and leaned against it for support. Unable to stay on my feet, I slid toward the concrete, the twinge in both wrists telling me I'd found the floor. I was out in seconds.

How long was I asleep? Another labored glimpse through the window revealed the alley in complete shadow. I figured it had to be mid-afternoon, maybe later. Although I still felt weak, the additional time had allowed my body to leach more of the drugs from my system, lifting the chemical cloud that had dulled my perception and fogged my memory. Ironically, the dissipation of the anesthesia also released me from a previously unappreciated side effect—a benevolent screen of indifference.

Since my abduction, I had experienced my circumstances remotely, like a bystander rubber-necking a grisly car wreck. Now I *knew* I was here, in the middle of it, unable to escape. And it filled me with the anxious conflict of wanting to know the truth, even though I was afraid it would confirm my worst suspicions.

I pushed away from the wall, the rough plaster an easy target for a rush of anger. Why were they treating me this way? Like a common criminal, a street thug. I'd committed no crime, nothing to warrant this kind of abuse. Maybe they had confused my identity with someone else—some rebellious hothead who had resisted the retrieval process.

I stared down at the cold, gray concrete. My innocent pretense was a poor replacement for the truth. Lying to myself, to keep the fear from becoming panic, to keep the terror from short-circuiting my ability to think and strategize, would not make the adjustment to my new life any easier. While I didn't have a grasp on the finer points, the big picture—the real reason I was here—was horrifyingly clear. And deluding myself was not going to change the facts. There was no Judas to blame. I had sold my soul knowingly. Willingly. And now the devil had come to collect.

How many others, I wondered, had been caught in the same headlights, rational their whole life, then something came along to make them lose their mind—for just an instant.

I tried to recall the man's name—the one I made the deal with. As best I could remember, he never bothered to introduce himself. No handshake. No smile. Only an invitation to sit.

At the time, I thought it was odd—the strange, almost comical scale of a tiny table with one chair set up in the middle of an abandoned warehouse—especially when there were four men. Agents, I assumed. All standing, waiting for me.

As I sat there, surrounded by the stench of rotting trash, my situation seemed so bizarre, so surreal, that the reality of what I was doing—the eventual consequences—didn't seem to be that important.

"You understand you're here by voluntary consent." It wasn't a question.

Now I realized it had been a warning, a critical disclosure meant to emphasize the gravity of what I was about to do, even though I was fairly certain the option of simply walking away was no longer available to me.

As I read through the contract, I was surprised at how short it was—three pages. I would have figured it took at least a dozen to sign your life away.

I asked about a clause in the fine print. *All rights of rescission irrevocably waived.* I asked because I thought it was funny, the kind of stuff I might read on the back of an invoice after buying aluminum siding from a door-to-door salesman.

His answer came quick, without hesitation. "It means that after you receive the goods, there's no going back, no changing the deal.

But remember, for six months, you can have anything you want, anything you can think of—travel, food, booze, pussy, you name it. It's yours."

Then the suit asked me if I had any more questions.

"Just one. What happens afterward? You know, after I get my six months?"

"There's a four day transition period. To get you ready. Then your continued life and liberty shall be at the discretion of the state."

"I'm not sure I understand what that means."

"It means you belong to *us*."

The tone of his voice was definite, final, and it made me flinch. He must have picked up on it, because he started right in on me. "You don't need to think about it. Just go for it. You could die tomorrow—die without the chance to enjoy any of it. It's not a bad trade, if you look at it in the right way."

And now, apparently, they had brought me here to do just that—to learn how to look at it in the right way.

Soon I would meet the man who would escort me to the final destination. It was one of the last things the suit told me as we were leaving the warehouse: When there were three days left, he would come.

I was on short time.

THREE

Day Zero
4:45 PM

"My name's Jake. Look man, it's nothing personal. I'm just here to do my job. So listen to me. You listening? Here's what I need you to do. Lay back on that mattress and relax. Eat when you're supposed to eat. Shit when you're supposed to shit. Stay quiet and don't ask no questions. You do exactly like I say and we'll get along fine."

His voice came low and steady and mostly free of slang, at least the kind I would have expected. His black face was hard and uneven, with odd shaped bulges under the skin, suggesting patches of steel plate and surgical epoxy. At over six feet and at least two hundred and fifty pounds, he looked as if he could snap a train in half if it would serve his purpose.

I decided to be as friendly as I knew how. Right from the start I would co-operate, try to be his buddy, convince him I was a team player. "I understand. I'm not going to give you any problems. You can count on it."

The big man had entered the room without warning. Impeccably dressed in a charcoal-gray tailored suit, I assumed the open collar and absence of a tie was intentional. A large gold ring set with a brilliant ruby stone strangled the small finger on his left hand—an anomaly of precious metal and jewel set against a gnarled ebony hand. I glanced under his jacket, searching for the tattletale strappings of a shoulder holster. From what I could see, he carried only a metal folding chair under one arm.

I waited for a response, some kind of confirmation that he understood. Instead, he jerked open the chair and tossed it in front of me. At first, I thought he wanted me to sit, but I quickly learned it was for his exclusive use. Kept outside the door, he brought it inside on his "visits," straddling it backward, the chair-back providing a mutually understood boundary between keeper and captive.

I kept silent, waiting for him to settle. He pulled out a small notepad and began to flip through the pages, as if hunting for something specific.

"You didn't eat much," he said.

I couldn't remember being hungry or even being offered anything to eat. "Must have been the drugs."

He nodded.

"So what's the deal?" I asked. "Do you know anything about my assignment—what they want me to do?"

No answer. He jotted a word or two in his notebook. His cell phone rang, breaking the awkward absence of conversation. The fact that he was allowed to bring a phone into the room surprised me. I took it as a good sign.

He took the call without a greeting, letting the other party speak first. Limiting his part of the exchange to a simple *yes* or *no*, it was over in twenty seconds.

He slipped the phone into his pocket and returned to his notes. I tried again. "You think they want me to work as some kind of special courier, like a mule, smuggling documents or some other stuff out of foreign countries? Is that what a lot of the other guys end up doing?"

He looked up at me. "What other guys?"

"You know, the others you watch, the ones who go into this program."

Jake's lips drew tight. After several seconds, I knew he wasn't going to answer me.

"Maybe they want me to be a kite," I prodded.

The huge man raised his eyes, a question mark contorting his features.

"I saw it in a movie once," I explained. "Where this government staffer called their agents *kites*, because if any of them ever got caught, they would be cut loose—let fly— without any kind of help. You think that's what they've got planned for me?"

Jake sat perfectly still, finally taking a deep breath before he spoke. "I don't think so."

He seemed more than sure.

"Well, they must have told you something about my assignment."

He didn't answer for the longest time, then said, "Didn't hear anyone use the word *assignment*."

"So what *did* they say?"

He gave me the kind of look he might give someone just before putting his gigantic fist through their face. "You'll get the details later. When you get off the plane."

"The plane? To where?"

He shook his head slowly. "No more questions."

"What difference does it make if you tell me?"

"Could make a lot of difference. Make you want to run. Make the next three days real . . . difficult."

His words left me more confused than afraid. I had accepted the idea that my new job was going to be dangerous. Even the drugged abduction hadn't really alarmed me. After all, this was deep-cover shit, black ops, and I figured it was the way things were done. But I was being treated like a prisoner, and Jake was turning out to be a tight-lipped jailor.

"Hey, I volunteered for this, remember? I thought we were on the same side, so what's with the attitude?"

He ignored me, preoccupied with the notebook he appeared to be using as a checklist. I gave it another shot, this time with less venom, wanting him to understand that I realized who was in charge. "I can't get out of here. That's obvious. And even if I did, I'm sure it's part of your job to track me down and bring me back."

He lifted his chin and I took it as a yes.

"So help me out. Give me something to go on. So I have some idea of what to expect."

He made a few more checkmarks in his little book, then tucked it away in a coat pocket. "You'll find out, when it's time. Right now, there's nothing else you need to know."

Jake and the chair seemed to stand at the same time. Our first meeting was over.

FOUR

Day One
6:45 AM

The acrid yellow light bounced off the floor, spreading over the walls like a coat of thick shellac. Another twenty-four hours had not diminished the room's dreary pallor. Its stark desolation made it seem more like a cage than a cell, and I worried that before it was all over, I would be down on my knees, crawling around on all fours.

I heard the ripple of a key being pushed into the door lock, followed by the solid snap of the bolt.

"You sleep?" Jake flipped open the chair and straddled it, his notebook already open.

"Some."

He made a note. "Need anything?"

"You kidding? I mean, come on, all I've got is this crappy mattress. What do *you* think?"

Jake stared at me with enough challenge to halt a charging rhino. He spoke slowly, placing intentional stress on each word. "I think you've forgotten our conversation from yesterday, so I'm gonna be real quiet for a few seconds and let you remember."

I waited long enough to suggest an effort to harness my attitude. "Okay, so you can't do anything about the accommodations, but there's gotta be plenty you can tell me."

He glared at me with exaggerated intensity—another warning not to push it. I took it down a notch. "I realize you probably took a loyalty oath or have to follow some straight-laced policy. I just want to find out what they have planned for me. I won't say anything, even if somebody asks me. There couldn't be anything wrong with that, right?"

"I got nothing to tell you, 'least nothing you wanna hear."

From his sheer size, Jake was intimidating as hell, yet I got the idea he wouldn't hurt me unless he absolutely had to. I decided to keep at him. "Look, Jake, maybe I made the wrong assumption. I thought you knew what was going on. But if you're just some kind of errand boy, working for the suits, doing what you're told—"

"What's it gonna take to get you to shut up?" Jake interrupted. "You're making this real hard on yourself, asking all these questions." He was studying me, surely picking up on the nervous twitches around my eyes, the forced strain along my jawline—the unconscious signs of fear.

I had to be careful, start over. "You're right. I've been pushing. Just imagine what it's like to be in my place."

"I don't need to imagine, 'cause I don't care."

I couldn't tell if his disposition conveyed disgust or indifference. He shifted backward in the seat, getting ready to leave.

The thought of spending another day with only doubt for company pushed me to near panic. I had to find a way to make him stay. I tried a different angle. "Is there anything you want to know about me?"

He cocked his head, exposing the braided ropes of muscle in his neck. "Everything I need to know is in the package."

"What package? What are you talking about?"

"*Your* package. Got everything inside—pictures, description, all the special stuff."

"What kind of special stuff?"

"Where you were born, how much schooling, if you had any kind of training, that sort of thing." Jake's words came with less reluctance, our discussion beginning to move back and forth without the guarded restriction he'd shown before.

"So what was in my package? What'd they tell you about me?"

His expression fell blank. "Don't remember anything special." He glanced at the floor then up at me, as if searching his memory. "Nope, nothing special about you."

I let it go, although later I would think it sad, living for nearly forty years and having done nothing worth remembering, nothing special.

"Maybe I need more time," I said. "With another ten years there's no telling what I might do." I smiled, trying to make it sound like a joke.

Jake scowled at me like I was some kind of pathetic beggar asking for a handout. Abruptly, he was on his feet, closing the notebook and collapsing the chair in the same instant—a show of synchronized yet restrained force. In seconds he was gone.

FIVE

Day Two
6:30 AM

I woke to find a small pot of coffee and a couple of sweet rolls sitting on the door's built-in food tray. I ate fast, thinking they wanted me ready, perhaps to meet with a supervisor to learn what kind of job they had planned for me. After what seemed like several hours, I chastised myself for not taking the time to enjoy the food, to have another cup of coffee while it was hot. Using the window as a makeshift sundial, I estimated the time to be around noon when I finally heard a key turn the lock.

"I've been ready all morning . . . just waiting." It sounded ludicrous, incongruent with my situation and surroundings.

"I know." Jake pointed to the air register mounted high on the wall.

"Camera?" I asked.

Jake nodded.

"See anything interesting?"

He squatted across the chair and began to flip through that damn notebook.

"Come on, Jake, you gotta give me something. I've been in this box for nearly three days now. What about a TV, a radio, anything that makes a noise?"

He ignored me.

"Okay, then how 'bout a little bull session?"

"We got nothin' to talk about." The attitude was back. Not as strong as before, but he was definitely on his guard.

"Tell me about your job. How long you been doing this? This part of it, I mean."

"This ain't a *part* of it. This is it."

"This is all you do, play nursemaid to a bunch of guys sitting in limbo?"

"I keep the package fresh, keep it from getting damaged before delivery."

"Doesn't sound like much of a career," I said. "You think you'll still be doing this in ten years?"

He blew out a breath. It was intentional—an overt gesture warning me to shut up. I didn't care.

"Jake?"

"Yeah," he growled. "I hear you."

"So what do you tell your kids when they ask you what you do at work?"

"Got no kids."

"No family?"

He didn't answer.

"Come on," I half-scolded. "Somebody raised you. Tell me what your parents were like."

He glared at me like he'd just caught me keying the paint on his car. He snapped his notebook closed. "You really wanna know? 'Bout my family?"

I offered a counterfeit smile. "I really do."

Jake hesitated, scanning the room. Although we both knew that others were listening, I wondered if this was a conversation he'd preferred to have in private. When his words finally came, he delivered them slow and steady, as if he'd memorized them from a script and didn't want to deviate from his last rehearsal. "I don't remember my mother. Only my father."

"So what was he like?"

"Tough. Tough with men, with women, with anybody that got in his way."

"Tough with you?"

The question seemed to throw him and his eyes fixed on my forehead as if he were focusing through the crosshairs of a gun-sight. "Suppose there's no reason not to tell you," he said, finally. "When I was 'bout eleven, I had this teacher who yelled at me. For not knowing the answer. She called me stupid. Too stupid to learn. Told me I shouldn't even be in school, said the better place for me was in the cotton field. That night I told my old man about it. He didn't say nothin', at least not then. Next morning, he told me he was going to class with me, talk to my teacher. I knew it was gonna be some bad shit, but I kept my mouth shut."

Jake paused, as if needing to suppress a rush of unresolved emotion from a memory that was better left in the past. I kept quiet, hoping to imply his feelings were more important than mine.

He pushed against the chair-back and straightened his shoulders, giving the indication he had regained control over his sudden and uncharacteristic vulnerability. "So we get to school and go inside the room and I sit in my seat like always. My old man's already walkin' up to her desk, where she's sitting real proper-like, working on stuff. At first, he stands right next to her, real close. She keeps asking him what he wants, but he don't say nothin'. Then, when she starts to squirm, when he sees her getting scared, he bends down and whispers in her ear. I see his lips moving, but I can't make out the words. The teacher, her face turns gray—that color you white people turn when all the blood drains out. Later on, after I get home, I asked him what he said. He told me straight out—that if she ever yelled at me again he would punch a hole in the back of her head and squeeze her brains like a sponge, wring all the stupid outta her."

I caught myself edging backward, biting the inside of my mouth, trying to camouflage my reaction.

"That teacher never said anything to me again. Never asked me a question, never even came near my dcsk. It was like I wasn't there. From then on, I figured that was the best way to be."

"What way?"

"Tough."

Jake bolted the door, locking me away for another day.

SIX

Day Two
8:15 PM

"You working a double shift?" I was wolfing down a plate of chicken and coleslaw. Jake's unexpected appearance put the brakes on my appetite. It was the first time he'd made a night call.

"Today you get two visits." He flipped open his pad and scanned the page. "And two visits tomorrow—your last day."

"Two? Why two? What's going on? What's the story?"

"Same story as always. You're here. You stay here. Until it's time."

"Then why the extra visits?"

"Procedure."

"Dammit Jake, I'm tired of these one word answers. I deserve to know something."

It was the first time I'd ever seen a look of surprise on his face, and it didn't last long.

"You don't deserve shit." His voice was thick with distain, like he was talking to a serial killer or child molester. "And what you got coming," he added, "you'll get soon enough."

There it was again—a reference to something ominous, something I wasn't going to like. "What do you mean by that? It's just a job, right? It might be a job nobody else wants—under-the-radar, covert stuff—but I'll be working for the government, right? So how bad could it be?"

He seemed to drift off in thought, the beginnings of a rogue smile slightly curling the edges of his mouth. "You know, I've always wondered if it would make a difference, if you knew what to expect before makin' the deal."

"Why? You think I would have changed my mind, turned it down?"

"You tell me. If you knew you were gonna be sitting in this rat-hole for the better part of a week, sweating it out 'til the last day, would all that fine food tasted as good? Would the pussy been as sweet? Or would something else— some worrying—always be diggin' at you, never leaving you alone, not letting you enjoy all that high livin' without having to think about the cost?"

I had always assumed he'd been playing with me, to see how rattled I'd get. Now I questioned if his constant allusions to some god-awful, sinister upshot was more than posturing—if the worst kind of future is what really waited for me. Because Jake didn't seem like the sort who joked around.

"I can't deny having second thoughts. I'm having plenty of them right now. And it's not helping me get through this. Look, I've asked you to cut me a break every time you come in here. I've done everything but beg. Is that what you want? You want me to beg?"

"Beg your ass off. Makes no difference to me."

"What *would* make a difference?"

He stared at me with the heartless consideration of an executioner deliberating between the merits of rope and electricity. "Sometimes I've wanted to tell. Like right now. So I could watch you fret over it. And then when I come in here for the last time, to strap you into the jacket, you could tell me if it made a difference." He paused, the measured control returning to his voice. "I think not knowing is going to worry you plenty. Make it real interesting. So you can just think about it, let it happen . . . like it's supposed to. And besides, day after tomorrow you travel." He was on his feet, snapping the chair closed.

"To where? Where am I going, Jake?"

He swung the door hard behind him, the bolt seating with a loud, metallic thud. He was done.

SEVEN

Day Three
4:50 AM

Sleep was impossible. Five minutes here, another ten there. I just kept waiting. For the sun to rise. For Jake to show up. I passed the time by trying to remember the names of the girls I'd slept with. I dug further, into my childhood, attempting to recall which toys I got on a particular Christmas.

I talked to the camera, hoping someone was listening. I told them about the woman I'd lived with for five years, and how she'd suddenly decided to move to Italy to study art or fashion or design—reasons that seemed vague and nebulous, yet compelling enough for her to explore the opportunity of a new life without me.

I rattled on, describing the boredom of working a crappy sales job year after year, telling them how I'd eventually decided to look for something better, something that would make me feel alive again. I told them about my vacations, where I'd been and the places I still wanted to see. I ended my soliloquy with some self-serving rhetoric about wanting to make the best of my situation, and how I hoped they would give me the chance. Although it carried the earmarks of an impromptu confession, I wanted them to learn as much as possible about the "package." The more they knew about me, the better my chances of scoring a sweeter deal.

The door finally opened mid-morning. I could tell Jake was agitated. I wondered if it had anything to do with me.

"So what's the plan for today?" I asked.

"No plan." Jake leaned the chair against the wall.

"So let's talk. You can tell me what's on the schedule for tomorrow. In a few hours, you're gonna tell me anyway. At least somebody is."

He looked like he might explode. "Right now your job is to wait. That's all. And you better start liking it, 'cause pretty soon that part is gonna be over, and then you'll wish you were back in this stinking shit-hole, 'cause it can go from bad to worse in a big hurry."

"It gets worse than this?"

"You thinkin' it would be different?" His scowl made it clear he would just as soon kick the crap out of me.

"Listen, Jake, you and I both know I'm not cut out for this. Maybe I can work a deal with the suits, pay them back. I've got a little money left, my pension, a small rental house in Boulder. I could make sure twenty percent goes to you, make it part of the deal."

He shook his head, indicating I'd said something stupid. "The suits done tore your life apart. You got nothin' left to bargain with. And besides, everything I need is at the other end of this phone." He patted his jacket pocket.

"Then tell me what comes next, what kind of future I've got."

Jake began to flip through his notebook, ignoring me, shutting me out.

I lowered my voice to a whisper. "I hid some cash offshore. Fifty grand. I can tell you how to find it."

Still nothing.

"You're not giving me a chance," I protested. "There must be something you want."

His huge frame stiffened, as if my words had released a paralytic toxin. "You got nothin' for me, you and the rest of your kind."

"My kind?" It came out as a challenge and I regretted it immediately.

"That's right, *your kind*." Jake's rising voice made it plain he wasn't to be interrupted. "Every one of you assholes comes in here thinkin' you're smarter than the last guy. Better. Deserving some kinda deal. But you're all the same. Just another one of those hard-starched, go-on-green-stop-on-red bastards that live in white town, following the rules, playing the game, living, breathing, and eating the same old shit day after day."

He waited, as if tempting me to argue. After a few seconds of silence, he asked, "Any of this sound familiar so far?"

I swallowed hard. "So far."

"Then something changes," he said. "Your woman leaves or you lose your job or some other shit happens and you think you got it bad. You start feeling sorry for yourself, go looking for some way to make it all better. And that's when the suits throw out the bait."

I couldn't believe how he knew, how he got it so absolutely right.

"Then you find your ass in here," he continued, "and you can't figure out how everybody suddenly turned on you—how they ain't your friend no more. A week ago you wanted a line of thousand dollar whores stretching to the horizon. But it's all different now. And tonight, when I come in here to tuck you in for the last time, you can bet your ass you won't be asking for any fine white pussy. You'll be wantin' me to turn my back, begging me to give you a five-minute head-start. So you listen to this, 'cause it's the only truth you're gonna hear. You had your play time, and now you got to pay the bill, make good on your part of the deal."

"But I don't know what my part of the deal is."

"It don't matter. At least not to me. 'Cause when you're screaming 'bout how you don't deserve any of this, I'll be down the road, on my way to some classy hotel where a couple of good-looking bitches are waitin' to ride me all night."

"What do you mean, *down the road?* You're turning me over to someone else?" Although I'd never thought of Jake as anything more than a glorified security guard, at least I *knew* him.

"When it's time for you to travel, somebody else gets the duty—somebody who hasn't heard all your whiney-ass crap and won't give a shit about how much you want out."

I wanted to believe he was making it all up. But his words were as black as his skin, tempered by the truth of someone who had been fucked with plenty. His matter-of-fact conviction told me he'd seen it in person— somebody else's hell—and it scared me shitless. He wasn't trying to persuade me to surrender and join ranks. He was simply telling me what was real—for him. And that I should realize it was about to become real for me.

"So if that's the way it is," I said, "if it's really that bad, why don't we cut the crap? I have a right to be told what's gonna happen to me. I deserve at least that much."

"You don't deserve shit."

"You're wrong!" I screamed. I could tell by the way his back went up I'd crossed the line. I didn't care.

Jake glanced at the air vent, into the camera. I'd forgotten others were watching. Maybe this was a test, to see how I would handle interrogation or psychological torture. Had the last two days been an evaluation, to see where I would best fit into the organization? It seemed a long shot at best.

I tried to calm down. I had to preserve my connection with Jake. Without it, I was completely cut-off, the four walls of my claustrophobic room offering the same freedom as a coffin. I blew out a breath, then regretted it, knowing it probably appeared melodramatic. "I didn't mean to fly off like that. I'm tired, and there's only a few hours left before I . . . travel."

Jake sneered. "Of all the things I ain't got for you, it's pity. If you're trying to make me feel sorry for you, you're wasting your time."

I started to answer, to tell him his sympathy was the last thing I wanted. Instead I nodded, deciding a subtle gesture—like the behavioral clues he'd no doubt been trained to recognize—would be more persuasive. But Jake was already moving toward the door, reaching for the chair he'd left leaning against the wall.

"Before you leave," I said, "there's something you need to know."

"Sounds more like something you need to say."

"Either way, I think it's important. You may want to sit down."

He hesitated. "Make it fast. I got stuff to do."

"There's a loose end. Something you don't know."

Jake jerked the chair open and assumed his usual straddle. "I don't think so."

"I'm serious," I insisted. "Something off the record. There's no way they could have found it."

Jake didn't try to hide his irritation. "Quit wasting my time. The suits know everything about you."

"I got family, somebody that might come looking for me."

"That's bullshit and we both know it. There's nobody given you a second thought in years."

"I've got a kid."

"Not according to the docs. Paperwork says you never had any kids."

"The records are wrong. Incomplete."

Jake shifted in his seat, restless, anxious to leave. "The suits check everything out. If there was a kid, it would be in the file."

"It was a long time ago. She was seventeen, had a year of high school left. I was in college. There was no way we could get married, raise a kid. She gave it up for adoption."

I paused, expecting more resistance from Jake. He was quiet, even distracted, apparently still listening. But not to me.

"Both of you gave up the kid?" Jake asked finally.

"Yeah." I shrugged my shoulders.

"Boy or girl?"

"It was a boy."

"You ever try to contact the kid? Check up on him?"

Somebody is feeding him questions. He's wearing an ear-bud. "It wasn't allowed."

"That's not what I asked. You ever contact him or not?"

"No, I thought it was best to stay out of his life."

Jake's inquiries were intentionally misleading. The suits had no interest in determining the amount of contact I'd had with the child during his infancy. Their real concern was that as an adult he might try to track down his biological father.

I was baiting him with another piece of the American dream gone bad. The story was true—and well concealed. And I knew at that very moment, state and county data banks were being scanned for an adoption certificate that would reveal my status as a paternal donor.

They wouldn't find it. Not under *my* name.

Jake squinted as the pallid light streaming through the window caught the side of his face. "What was the mother's name?"

"Lisa. Lisa Saunders." I wondered how long it would take.

"You both lived in the same town?"

"Yeah, a couple miles apart."

"When was the last time you talked to her?"

I waited, as if struggling to remember. "It's been years, not since—"

Jake's flinch was nearly imperceptible, and if I hadn't been watching closely, I would have missed it. It was his cell phone, vibrating.

"Yeah?" The call lasted less than ten seconds. Jake snapped the phone shut and dropped it back into his pocket. His part of the conversation had been limited to a single word. He looked up at me with rapt attention. "Convince me."

They'd found the adoption cert! They knew I wasn't lying. Perhaps just as significant, the call had come from the outside, from a higher level of authority than resided within this holding complex. Otherwise it would have been relayed through Jake's earpiece. Now I had something to negotiate with, something the suits might feel was valuable enough to trade for information.

"There's a lot more."

"I don't have all day. Let's hear it." Jake was impatient, demanding.

"No way. First you tell me what I want to know, and then I'll give you—"

"You're talking, but nobody's listening," Jake interrupted.

"Sure they are. Maybe for the first time. I imagine that little ear-bud of yours is buzzing like a wet hornet's nest."

Jake rose slightly off the seat, his clothes appearing to stretch as his muscles responded to an increased flow of adrenalin. "Listen asshole, you need to get with the program. You're not in a position to be demanding shit."

I knew he could beat it out of me or use drugs to lower my resistance. I wasn't ready to give in. Not yet.

"I'm asking, like a gentleman," I countered. "I'm suggesting a business proposition. We trade information. I give you want you want, and you do the same for me."

Jake's forehead contorted into a mass of creases and bulging veins. "You've been a pain in the ass since you got here, and I'm getting real tired of putting up with your attitude."

He was posturing, trying to intimidate me with a veiled threat of force. I blocked it out. "The suits can't find the other half of the records." My voice was cocksure, almost arrogant. "Without it, you don't know who raised the kid or what happened to him. They've already searched and come up with zilch. You know it. I know it. Otherwise you wouldn't still be talking to me."

"You gotta give me something," he growled. "Something that counts. Enough for the suits to believe you've got real gen."

What I said next would no doubt be analyzed by a battery of experts. Although their evaluation would be focused on verifying hard facts, they would also be appraising my willingness to support—and perhaps join—a team that offered its members unassailable immunity in exchange for selfless allegiance.

At best, they would judge me to be a worthwhile asset, someone to be groomed for high-level work. The downside was equally plausible. I could wake up strapped to a bed, straining to focus through a lingering haze of drug-induced intoxication, my memories already transcribed and backed-up on the agency's mainframe.

In spite of the risk, I had managed to put the possibility of full disclosure on the table, and now I had the chance to play out my hand.

"It was a long time ago," I began. "I was twenty."

"Who else knew?"

"Her mother. I don't know who else she might have told. It wasn't something the family wanted advertised. We kept it quiet."

"You're sure? No heart-to-heart with a best friend?"

"Neither one of us wanted the stigma. Lisa moved out of state, lived in special housing set up by the agency. The adoption was a private placement. She got more money that way, enough to live on for a year. They paid for everything. Medical, transportation, the works."

Jake's attention was locked on, as if there was a piece of food on my upper lip and he couldn't take his eyes off it. He was looking for a tell, a little twitch or a rapid blink, an indication I was lying.

"At first," I continued, "I stayed in touch with Lisa's mother. That didn't last long."

Jake turned his head slightly. I realized he was listening to research updates. "Her mother's dead." He said it as a matter of fact, and yet I could imagine some intel-analyst sitting in an office at the Pentagon or Langley, crossing her off the list with an undercurrent of relief—one less thing to worry about.

"And her father?" I didn't really care, but it seemed like the right thing to do, to ask.

"VA med center. Alzheimer's."

"What about Lisa? Have you tracked her down?"

Jake hesitated as new information was relayed through his earpiece. "She's gone. Eight years ago. Car accident."

It was a possibility I'd never considered. Unaffected, I felt a twinge of guilt over letting the news just flow through me, giving it no more consideration than I would yesterday's weather report.

"I guess that leaves me." I was hoping to hammer home the new clout I'd inherited. Unfortunately, it sounded like I was admitting to being the last surviving carrier of some virulent disease—and easy to eradicate. "So what else do you want to know?" I braced for it. I knew exactly what they were after. I had to hold back. The last piece of information was my insurance, my last bargaining chip, and I couldn't give it away without their agreement to disclose the details of my assignment.

"What was the name of the family who adopted the baby? Where'd they live? The suits want everything you have on them."

There it was—my hole card. I sat back against the wall, my palms flat on the mattress. I had to keep Jake from seeing it on my face or in the twitch of a finger. If I kept my body tense, my muscles tight, there would be less chance of him noticing that I was as scared as I was determined.

The adoption had been handled by a church-sponsored quasi-agency, where prospective parents with money could buy privacy and discretion. In this stratified arena of negotiated birthright, the separation between child and birth parents was designed to be permanent, to prevent the biological and sometimes latently remorseful parents from initiating contact with their discarded offspring. Details of the adoptive parents were obscured by multiple layers of intentionally confusing bureaucracy—a complex organization of shill companies and paper corporations—providing greater assurance that the adoption would not become a matter of public record. To penetrate this well-constructed veneer of secrecy would require substantial effort—and time. While certainly not beyond the ability of the intelligence operatives who researched and investigated intentionally cloaked information, it could take several days before they discovered the child had died before his second birthday.

SHORT TIME

The only reason I knew about the infant's early demise was due to the required health notification sent by the agency, advising of the likelihood of a congenital heart defect in one or both parents. At the time, my few moments of grieving over a child I'd never seen was selfishly followed by a battery of diagnostic tests to confirm the reliability of my own heart.

From the nature of Jake's interrogation, I knew the suits had hit a wall. Although they'd found the adoption certificate, it had been completed in counterpart, and only the section that released maternal rights had been filed in state records. The portion of the document containing the identity of the adoptive parents was never recorded. The agency had not discovered—yet—the point of entry into a labyrinth of convoluted data, most of it salted with straw parties, post office boxes, and Utah-based corporations. Eventually, their efforts would reveal the child's ill-fated destiny. But right now, as far as they knew, he was alive. And as a young adult, he represented a potential problem—an adoptee who might decide to track down his sole biological parent.

"The names of the adoptive parents were kept private. I can tell you how to find out who they are."

Jake waited a few seconds. "So tell it."

"I'm not giving you any more information. Not until you brief me on my assignment, my new job." I did my best to show my determination without appearing obstinate. I had already decided that if things got nasty, I could make some vague reference to a religious organization that provided adoption services for wealthy parishioners. Right now I would hold on to what little leverage I had for as long as I could.

Jake was quiet for several seconds. I expected he would come back strong, threaten to tear my head off if I didn't finish the story. His response surprised me—his voice was measured, almost solemn. I didn't like it. It reminded me of someone speaking at a funeral, the insights coming much too late to be appreciated by the deceased.

"Right now," he began, "the suits need you. They got a plan. But the second you turn high maintenance, they'll pull out the contract and read you the fine print. And afterwards, you won't have the same value. You'll be a piece of baggage, slowing everybody down."

It was more than a cryptic threat. It was an ultimatum. As I tried to imagine what they might do to me, Jake reached for his cell phone, this time to make a call rather than answer one. He watched me with obvious expectation. "You need to be thinking about this. Hard." He punched one, maybe two numbers—presets—and held the phone to his ear.

Had I pushed too far? Was this another test? Who was Jake talking to? How much authority did they have? Was their decision irreversible? A surge of panic told me I was throwing away any chance of getting out of this room with my brain function registering above the level of a cabbage.

Jake mumbled something. I couldn't hear it. Now he was listening—getting instructions, orders. It might be too late.

I blurted it out, desperately needing to interrupt his conversation. "Put it away. The kid's dead."

Jake moved the phone away from his ear. Several discordant tones confirmed the movement of his thumb on the keypad as he terminated the call. He had won. It didn't feel that way. Instead of regret, I sensed the liberation of an eleventh hour reprieve, the relief of being granted a last minute stay of execution.

I gave him every detail I could remember, even spelling the name of the congregational church that had initially handled the arrangements. By the time I finished, Jake was eyeing me with unusual, even curious scrutiny.

"Not bad."

"What, are you saying you enjoyed that?"

"You think you're the first to try to bluff your way out of here?"

"I wasn't really—"

"Yeah, right. Most make it up as they go along. No real story. Full of holes. But yours smelled good, especially at the beginning. That's when you gotta grab the suits, at the very beginning."

In his own strange way, he was paying me a compliment. Cat and mouse. Hide and seek.

"Am I supposed to learn something from this?" I asked. "Something I can use on the outside?"

Jake stood and left the chair. He walked to the window and pressed his huge hand against the reinforced glass, as if testing it, confirming it was secure. "I've decided."

"Decided what?"

"To tell you."

I had to make sure we were talking about the same thing. "You mean about my job, how the suits are going to use me?"

"Yeah. Even before your bullshit story about the kid, I was thinkin' about it. Now I'm sure. And it ain't gonna be no fairytale.

Whether it was Jake's decision to make or he'd been given permission to reveal the details of my immediate future, his reversal of logic confused me. There was something menacing, even sinister, in his *wanting* to tell me. Yet I didn't want to sidetrack him. "I appreciate that." It sounded hollow, insincere.

"You might. You might not. We'll see."

Another dark reference to my future, insinuating that revealing it would be its own kind of punishment. I didn't care. He was going to tell me, and I wanted to know.

"Maybe you'll surprise me," Jake continued. "Maybe you'll take it different than the others, show me what kind of man you are."

"Yeah, maybe." My stomach was squeezing its contents into my throat. I took a few deep breaths. I prayed.

Jake returned to his seat, settling in against the metal backrest. "You and I both know you messed up bad. But there's no changing the past. And now you got to figure out how to deal with it until the night man comes in here to shoot you up."

They had already drugged me once, so the promise of additional sedatives didn't surprise me. I lowered my head. "Thanks for telling me." It sounded contrived, too polite for the surroundings. For some reason, Jake didn't take it that way.

"So you and I are real clear," he said, speaking slower than usual. "I got nothin' to do with it. Like I said in the beginning, it's just my job to get you there in one piece. Nothin' personal, you understand?"

As far as I was concerned, it was *all* personal, but I kept my mouth shut.

"They'll come for you in the morning around five. You'll fly most of the day, but you won't know it."

"The drugs?"

He nodded. "Easier that way. Next day, they turn you over to the locals. You wait an hour, maybe two. They take some pictures, our people get a receipt for the delivery. Then you pay the bill, even things up."

I interrupted him before he could start his next sentence. "What bill? What kind of payment? For what?"

Jake shot me a cold, pathetic stare, the way a judge scrutinizes the condemned before handing down his sentence. "You need to shut up and listen. Otherwise, come five o'clock tomorrow, you're still gonna be sitting on that floor, bitchin' about how the world doesn't play by your rules."

"I'm sorry." I held my hands up in front my chest. "I'll be quiet. I promise."

Jake sat there, letting me squirm, punishing me for my outburst. Finally, he spoke. "Here's how it went down, at least it's the way I heard it. One of our guys from the State Department was tooling around in his Jag. Top's down, he's got his foot on it. Then this ankle-biter runs out in front of him. There's no way he can stop. He turns the kid into a pinball, bouncing him off a tree or two before he goes flat. Seems the kid belongs to some big shot oil sheik, and when daddy finds out his boy got turned into a hockey puck, he gets real pissed."

"So what's that got to do with me?"

"The camel jockey wants justice. He wants somebody's balls floatin' in his soup bowl. But the bad guy—the one driving the Jag—been giving head to the suits for years and they owe him, right? So the word comes down from high up in the department, says he gets protection, we're not giving him up. Instead they offer money, thinking the problem will go away. But daddy-sheik already got more money than he can spend, and he turns the spigot on a big pipeline full of oil. So you can imagine the kind of shit he's threatening if he doesn't get the sap who trounced his kid. Get the picture? He wants revenge, payback for killing his son."

I was getting a bad feeling—even worse than the nausea I was fighting—about how this story was going to turn out. Yet I wasn't ready to admit that some third world oil sheik's dead kid had anything to do with me. "Okay, so how do I fit into all of this?"

"So the suits gotta give him somebody."

"What do you mean . . . somebody?"

"Jesus, don't you get it? You're gonna take the rap. The suits gonna turn you over to this pissed off sheik. They gonna tell him you were the one driving the Jag."

"I've never been in a Jag."

"You have now. And you don't remember what happened 'cause you were drunk when you bounced that kid off your bumper."

I gaped at him like he'd been speaking a foreign language. It must've shown because he immediately reminded me of the meeting that took place in that empty warehouse a little over six months ago. "Hey, it's the deal you made. And tomorrow, they're gonna ship your ass east—way east—as a peace offering."

"For a trial?"

"Trial?"

"Yeah, you know, a trial, with lawyers and a judge."

"Haven't you been listening to me? Fuck the trial, man. You're bought and paid for."

I pulled my knees tight against my chest. My head was suddenly heavy and I let it fall forward, catching it in my hands. I didn't care that Jake could see me breaking into a clammy sweat. Finally, I mumbled, "So then what happens? Do they take me out and shoot me?"

He lips drew thin as his mouth contorted into a grimace. "Not that easy."

I could hear my breathing fill the room— quick shallow drafts as my stomach threatened to spasm. I leaned forward on my knees, not wanting to vomit on the mattress. "Just tell me," I whispered, hoping he could hear me.

"I seen it done. Couple of times. They turn it into a real circus. Chain you down in the public square, beat on some drums, wave some flags. There's usually TV cameras, lots of banners and shit. Then they run over your ass, use your guts as party favors."

"Run me over?" I said it without thinking— needing an explanation, but not ready to hear it.

"They do this kind of crazy wack all the time. It's their way. To get payback, settle the score."

Part of me wanted to call him a liar. Yet if the sheer terror tugging at my insides was any indication, I was buying every word. Until an hour ago, I had thought of Jake as a simple hired hand, putting in his time, doing his job. Now he was part of the process, hammering it home, making me believe.

"It won't come quick," he added. "They use a half-track. They'll make that thing crawl over you real slow, draw it out, a few inches at a time."

I tried to shut down, turn off my brain. It was impossible. I kept hearing the words, seeing the image—a man chained to the hot asphalt, his arms and legs straining against inflexible links of steel, and a few feet away, a huge military vehicle belching black diesel exhaust, its path and purpose an insane yet indisputable certainty.

I asked the only thing I could think of. "You'll shoot me full of drugs so I don't feel it, right?"

"Can't. They pull your blood and test it. Make sure you're clean. Only thing you can do is deal with it. No matter how long it takes, you'll just have to deal with it."

I was on the verge of passing out. I fought to keep my balance. The space beneath me changed color, then texture. I shut my eyes, thinking it was odd to worry about where I would sleep now that my shitty little mattress was saturated with puke.

I wanted Jake to leave. I wanted to hear the *click-clack* of the collapsing chair, the dead metallic thud of the door seating against the jamb, the bolt snapping into place.

Regardless of the motivation—a superior's mandate or because he had more to say—Jake stayed. As my head began to clear, I looked up and saw him still straddling the chair, dissecting me with an expression of deep satisfaction.

With my stomach emptied of its contents, the numbing shock turned to anger. Although it would have been easy to direct it at Jake in retaliation for his voyeuristic addiction to watching others suffer and rot away with fear, I knew it was one of the reasons he had the job. Outside this complex, his penchant for sadistic pleasure would have made him a social deviant. But here, inside this specially created hell, it made him a rare and valuable asset. I had to see past his perversions because, good or bad, he was my only source of information, and what he had told me didn't make any sense.

My own government was going to hand me over to a foreign country, a country ready to kill me for a crime I didn't commit. "Our people . . . they really do this kind of shit?"

"All the time."

"But what about my rights? What about the law? How can they just write me off, let me die for something I didn't do?"

Jake dropped his eyes and for the longest moment stared at the floor. Finally he said,

"Go to sleep." Without another word, he snapped up the chair and left.

EIGHT

Day Three
11:50 PM

I heard the door open. The huge figure was backlit by the hallway fluorescents and I knew immediately it was Jake. I could tell he was carrying something. For an instant, I thought he was bringing me another dinner to replace the one I'd lost. He switched on the light, letting me see.

I instinctively began shaking my head. "You don't need to use those. I don't have anywhere to run."

"Running's only part of it," he said. "I gotta keep you from hurting yourself. Keep *me* from having to hurt you, 'cause you make me chase your ass. They want you perfect. They wanna do all the damage—right from the start."

I glanced at the four leather-lined metal shackles tethered by short lengths of chain. "You taking me now?"

"You got about five hours."

"Then I'm asking you, in the only way I know how . . . don't put those on me. Not yet. I need to move around, pretend I'm free right up to the last minute. When I have to leave, you can put them on. I want to spend the rest of my time alone, thinking, getting my head straight."

The intimidation in Jake's eyes was more than a warning. "You're not gonna fuck with the night man?"

"I swear to God . . . absolutely not."

"If you screw with him, especially after I give you a break, it will go down twice as hard. You understand?"

I couldn't imagine anything twice as bad as being run over with a half-track, but I had to convince Jake that I would co-operate. "No problem. I won't do anything stupid. You can check on me later if you want."

"It won't be me. I'm done." Jake turned to leave.

I realized this was the last time I would see him. "Wait! Can you give me a minute?"

"What for? I got plans, remember?"

"I got a question. And there's nobody else I can ask. It'll just take a second. I promise."

He leaned against the door, the chain restraints dangling from his arms. "Make it quick."

"You said you'd seen it done. I need to know what to expect."

He frowned. "It won't make any difference, not any easier."

"I want to hear it."

Jake turned and opened the door. I was sure he was leaving. Outside, I heard the metallic crash of a hundred links of welded steel hit the floor. I hoped he was trading the chain for the folding chair. It would have been familiar, comfortable. Instead, he resumed his stance in front of the door.

"Couple of hours before sunrise," he began, "several guards will come for you. They'll put you in a truck and drive you to a square in the center of town. Then they'll drag you to the middle of the street and chain you to iron rings fixed in concrete. There'll be people waiting— a big group—and they'll push forward to surround you. At first the guards will pretend to hold them back. Then they'll let some of them through, for the cameras. The men scream curses and the women spit. A few will kick and stomp on you, but not hard enough to do any real damage."

"Because they're saving me for the big finish?"

Jake's eyes were cold and vacant.

"When it's time," he continued, "they bring the half-track up, stopping it a foot or so away. They'll start with your feet. Then it's just gettin' it over with."

"How long?"

"Fifteen minutes. Sometimes more."

Numbing tentacles of shock prevented me from reacting. My lack of response must have disappointed him.

"Did it help?" he asked.

I knew my next words would be the last thing I would ever say to Jake—the final time I would speak to this contradiction of cold-hearted antagonist and friend of last resort. But I had nothing to say, or maybe nothing worth saying, and I shook my head.

SHORT TIME

Without hesitating, he turned, opened the door and slipped out.

NINE

Time To Travel
3:15 AM

There was no more sleep, only the light drone of the air handler murmuring through the vent. Yesterday, Jake had returned my watch. Now I knew why—so I could count the hours. To leave me guessing would have been cruel even by Jake's compassionless standards.

The familiar metallic ripple of a key sliding into the lock brought raw nerves to the surface. It was much too soon. And I needed every last second. Because they were mine—and they were all I had left.

A huge black hand wrapped around the edge of the door. A pinpoint glint of crimson light flashed from one of the fingers.

"Jake? What are you doing here? What's going on? Is it time? Is the guy here with the drugs?" The words shot from my mouth as I stumbled to my feet.

"Slow down. I need you to listen."

"You told me I wasn't going to see you again. You said somebody else would come for me. Are you going to be the one who takes me? Do you have to put the chains on me now?"

"Shut the fuck up."

I thought about rushing him, hitting him full force with all my weight. If I could push him off balance and make it into the hallway, there might be a chance I could find my way outside. Maybe there would be somebody on the street, somebody who would listen. A witness.

"The suits wanna offer you a deal," he said. "You got another chance."

A deal. Another chance. I heard the words, but they weren't registering.

"You hear me?" Jake asked. "You got a way out. And you gotta decide right now."

"What are you talking about? You told me the decision was made and there was nothing I could do."

"Things have changed. And if you want the new deal, you gotta listen. And one more thing. You'll have to give up your last day—tomorrow—if you wanna make the switch."

"What switch? With who?"

"The suits got themselves a situation. They need somebody for a job, a white man about your size. And they need him tonight."

"So they asked for me?" Maybe someone had finally realized that I had value, enough to redeem me from my fate as a condemned surrogate.

"They don't care who it is. I got the call, they told me to handle it, make the choice. I thought I'd ask you first, before I—"

"Does that mean some other poor bastard takes my place?" I interrupted.

"You or somebody else, makes no difference to me."

"You're saying all I have to do is tell you I wanna make the switch?"

"And you take the new deal," Jake said. "But I gotta know now. You got the shortest time, one day left, and you'd have to give it up . . . if that's what you decide."

"So, no half-track? No spreading my guts all over the street?"

He shook his head. "Nothin' like that."

"You know about the new deal?" I knew he did. He had to. He'd told me about the envelopes, full of pictures and details.

This time there was no hesitation. "One of our agents dropped off the map, trying to score early retirement. Took a lot of cash with him. You take his place and wc put the money back. Real simple. Everything's back to normal."

"What about this guy's family, his friends? Even if the suits do cosmetic surgery on me, I'll never look exactly like him." Then I remembered. "Oh, wait. You guys don't have friends. No family. Right?"

He nodded slowly. "Right."

"So that means I'd be working a straight job for the government. Kinda like you, right?

"If you want it, I gotta call it in. Otherwise they'll take someone else."

I wanted it like a drowning man wants another breath of air. "Yeah, sure. It sounds fine. I'd leave tonight?"

"Right now."

"Where will I be working?"

"The agent was outta San Francisco."

"Probably went to Mexico, the bastard. So I would take his place? Be an agent, undercover, carrying heat, fucking with some mark's brain? You know, the same way you fucked with mine?"

"You'd take the guy's place."

Ten minutes ago I was condemned to die. Now I was being offered a new life. A reprieve. A chance to make it work. "Okay, let's do this."

"You sure?"

"I'm ready. I want out of here."

"I brought your stuff." Jake pointed to a small bag he'd dropped by the door.

The door. For the first time, he'd left it open. I wouldn't have to run. They were letting me go. I was really leaving.

I walked over, bent down, and retrieved the bag. "I think I'm going to like San Francisco. I've only been there once, but I remember—"

The .40 caliber's external suppressor released the bullet in near silence. There was no flash from the muzzle and only the solid metallic snap of the bolt pushing another round into the barrel confirmed the weapon's operation. A half-second later, the empty brass hit the floor with a hollow ring, rolled a few inches, and stopped at Jake's shoe. He reached down, picked up the spent shell and put it in his pocket.

The following afternoon, the San Francisco Chronicle carried a brief story about the unfortunate death of a customs and immigration official involved in a single car accident. The body, burned beyond recognition, was identified by state-furnished dental records. The deceased left no family, and no funeral service was scheduled.

Author's Note

For those readers who are wondering why the unfortunate protagonist's name was never revealed . . .

I decided early on in the writing of *Short Time* to leave him unnamed. Rather than focus on a specific albeit fictional individual, I wanted to represent a composite of the many unheralded countrymen and citizens who, for reasons both good and bad, find themselves in circumstances and situations which inevitably result in their ultimate sacrifice. And while disastrous for them personally, their actions arguably serve a larger purpose—perhaps the greater good. Since the nature of their deeds prevent history from revealing the significance of their contribution, the identity of these quasi-heroes must also remain a well-guarded secret.

About the Author

Jaye Frances is the author of seven books including *The New Girl in Town* and the suspense thriller trilogy, *World Without Love*. Her other published works include *The Beach*, *The Kure*, and *Love Travels Forever*. Storyteller, truth-seeker, and optimist, Jaye explores relationships, philosophy, and the complexities of life—a day at a time.

For more info, visit:

JayeFrances.com
JayeFrancesBooks.com
JayeFrancesYouTube.com
JayeFrances.Substack.com
LinkedIn.com/in/JayeFrances
Facebook.com/JayeFrancesAuthor
Twitter.com/JayeFrancesNews
Instagram.com/JayeFrancesWriter
Goodreads.com/author/show/5232105.Jaye_frances

Books by Jaye Frances
World Without Love Series

Betrayed
Book One - World Without Love

Reunion
Book Two - World Without Love

Redemption
Book Three - World Without Love

Available in eBook and Paperback from Amazon

The New Girl in Town
And Other Journeys Above and Below the Belt

The Beach
Including the Novella, Short Time

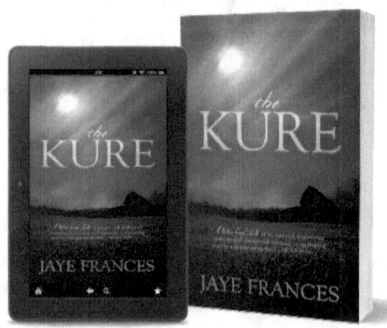

The Kure

Love Travels Forever

~~~

Jaye Frances Books are Available in eBook and Paperback at JayeFrancesBooks.com

World Without Love - The Series
Betrayed – Reunion - Redemption
Betrayed
Book One - *World Without Love*

Jewel has everything going for her—a handsome husband, a promising future, and lots of time to explore an island paradise she now calls home. But when a group of strangers accompanies her husband home for a friendly game of poker, her life quickly becomes a hellish nightmare of deceit and betrayal.

Now her very survival depends on entering a world where sex, domination, and money are inseparable, where women must obey all masters, and where every desire has its price.

World Without Love contains mature content and is intended for an 18+ audience

Betrayed is available in eBook and paperback at

BetrayedBookOne.com

Reunion
Book Two - *World Without Love*

In **Reunion**, Jewel's story continues as she finds herself stranded in a far-flung corner of the world. Struggling to elude her captors and a network of bounty hunters, she meets her would-be savior, a man who promises to provide protection and comfort. Believing her nightmare has finally come to an end, Jewel begins making plans to return home, where she can start her life over again.

But greed raises its ugly head, and the terrifying future she thought she'd evaded becomes a reality. Deceived by the only one she believed she could trust, Jewel is left defenseless against the sadistic abusers who take pleasure in teaching her their own form of discipline. With the dream of rescue and returning home to San Diego even further from her reach, she begins planning her revenge on the men who have stolen her life—and her future.

World Without Love contains mature content and is intended for an 18+ audience.

Reunion is available eBook and paperback at
ReunionBookTwo.com

Redemption
Book Three - *World Without Love*

Rescued from Bangkok's evil flesh markets, Jewel's victory over her captors is bittersweet. Haunted by her last memories of Annie, Jewel vows to do whatever it takes to find her friend—hopefully in time to save her from a sadistic killer. Using her new position as an embassy hostess, Jewel begins to form alliances with the constant stream of visiting political attaches and power brokers, hoping one of them can help find Annie—still alive.

Quick to recognize Jewel's special assets, her supervisors offer her more responsibility, and with it, the benefits of unsupervised travel and the latitude to call her own shots in the completion of her duties. No longer under the scrutiny of the all-seeing covert government network, Jewel realizes she has been given another special privilege, one that her superiors could not have anticipated—the freedom to extract revenge on all those who attempted to destroy her life.

But again, the hand fate touches Jewel's heart. And before she can stop herself, a professional relationship becomes very personal, forcing her to choose between the man she loves and the one who helped her escape a dismal world of enslavement and cruel domination.

World Without Love contains mature content and is intended for an 18+ audience

Redemption is available in eBook and paperback at
RedemptionBookThree.com

World Without Love – **The Complete Series**
Includes ***Betrayed, Reunion, and Redemption***

In ***Betrayed***, Jewel has everything going for her—a handsome husband, a promising future, and lots of time to explore an island paradise she now calls home. But when a group of strangers accompanies her husband home for a friendly game of poker, her life quickly becomes a hellish nightmare of deceit and betrayal. Now her very survival depends on entering a world where sex, domination, and money are inseparable, where women must obey all masters, and where every desire has its price.

Jewel's story continues in ***Reunion***, as she finds herself alone and stranded in a far-flung corner of the world. Struggling to elude her captors and the network of bounty hunters, she meets her would be savior, a man who promises to provide protection and comfort. Jewel believes her nightmare has finally come to an end. But greed raises its ugly head, and the terrifying future she thought she'd evaded becomes a reality—one that seems impossible to escape.

In the final chapter, ***Redemption***, Jewel is rescued from Bangkok's evil flesh markets by a covert government agency. Haunted by her last memories of Annie, Jewel vows to do whatever it takes to find her friend—hopefully in time to save her from Gregory's sadistic and murderous intentions. In her new position as an embassy hostess, Jewel forms alliances with political attaches and power brokers, hoping one of them can help her find Annie—still alive.

World Without Love contains mature content and is intended for an 18+ audience

World Without Love–**The Complete Series** is available in eBook at **WorldWithoutLove.com**

The New Girl in Town
And Other Journeys Above and Below the Belt

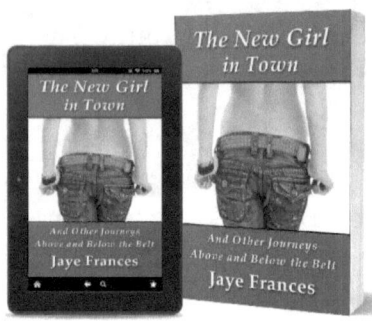

This special collection contains nine of Jaye's most heart-wrenching, mind-tingling, titillating, and thought-provoking stories. Here's a glimpse of what's inside …

- **Our Girl** – Every town has one, and there's always one guy who wants her for his own
- **Three Conversations** – Hindsight often brings wisdom, self-discovery, and a sense of closure—unless the heartache is too much to bear.

- **My First Girlfriend** – There's nothing like a first experience, especially when it brings respect, admiration, and unconditional surrender.

- **The Family Business** – Like mother, like daughter. Until the situation creates a dangerous legacy – and things have to change.

- **The Sighting** – Coming face-to-face with an urban myth can be exciting – and frightening. But when the truth reveals a surprise no one saw coming, it's time for a whole new perspective.

- **Avocados and Fruit Salad** – New beginnings are all around us, if we're willing to recognize the opportunities and take a few risks

- **Younger by Ten** – When love is about the numbers, a few hearts are bound to be broken, especially when you realize your choice of lover had nothing to do with you.

- **A Lie I Desperately Want to Believe** – Trust is often part of the collateral damage when the unquestioning bond of marriage is ripped to shreds.

- **The New Girl in Town** – Sometimes it takes a while to figure out what you want – and build the confidence to go for it!

The New Girl in Town is available in eBook and paperback at **TheNewGirlBook.com**

The Beach

Alan loves the beach. More than a weekend respite, it is his home, his refuge, his sanctuary. And for most of the year, he strolls the sand in blissful solitude, letting nature—and no one else—touch him. But spring has given way to summer, and soon, the annual invasion of vacationers and tourists will subdivide the beach with blankets, umbrellas, and chairs, depriving Alan of his privacy and seclusion—the fundamental touchstones of his life.

Resigned to endure another seasonal onslaught of beach-goers, Alan believes there is nothing he can do but prepare for the worst.

But fate has other plans.

Delivered to him on the crest of a rogue wave, the strange object appears to have no purpose, no practical use—until Alan accidentally discovers what waits inside. Now he must attempt to unravel an ageless mystery, unaware that the final outcome will change his life, and the beach, forever.

In the companion novella **Short Time,** you'll meet a respectable but bored middle-class executive, who exchanges his future for six months of excess and extravagance, only to discover out the price he must pay for his hedonistic indulgence is beyond anything he could have imagined.

The Beach is available in eBook and paperback
at **BewareTheBeach.com**

Love Travels Forever

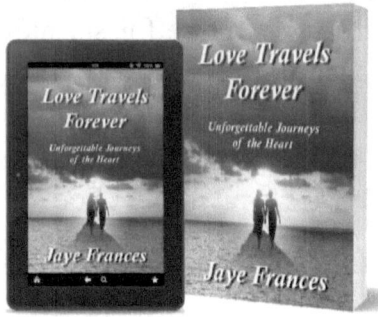

In **Love Travels Forever**, Jaye Frances captures the reader's heart with an inspiring collection of seventeen stories filled with romance and passion, the hopeful innocence of youth, and a love so strong that it transcends the mortality of life. Here are just a few of the people you'll meet:

Evan and Frankie, a loving couple traveling through life hand-in-hand, are unaware that the shadow of fate is about to tear them apart. Helpless to change their shortened future together, one of them makes a promise—a promise of devotion and courage, honoring a love that surpasses the boundaries of time.

Mark and Janice, the perfect couple with the perfect life, are on the threshold of finally seeing their dreams come true—until an unexpected circumstance changes their lives forever.

Danny, a young soldier fresh out of boot-camp, is desperate to find a way to travel home and marry his sweetheart before being shipped overseas. Stranded in a train station on a three day pass with no hope in sight, Danny meets Wanda, an incredible woman who vows to find a way to bring Danny and his fiance together.

Nora and Georgia are two eight-year-old best friends who share giggles, dolls, and secrets. But when one of them faces sudden danger, the other responds with an unconditional act of love and forges a lifelong bond between them unaffected by fear or prejudice.

So find a quiet spot, get comfy, and grab a box of tissue. You're about to take an unforgettable journey of the heart, to a place where compassion and hope have no limits, and where love continues to travel forever.

Love Travels Forever is available in eBook & paperback at **LoveTravelsForever.com**

The Kure

John Tyler, a young man in his early twenties, awakens to find a ghastly affliction taking over his body. When the village doctor offers the conventional, and potentially disfiguring, treatment as the only cure, John tenaciously convinces the doctor to reveal an alternative remedy—a forbidden ritual contained within an ancient manuscript called the *Kure*.

Although initially rejecting the vile and sinister rite, John realizes, too late, that the ritual is more than a faded promise scrawled on a page of crumbling paper. And as cure quickly becomes curse, the demonic text unleashes a dark power that drives him to consider the unthinkable—a depraved and wicked act requiring the corruption of an innocent soul.

The Kure contains mature content and is intended for an 18+ audience

The Kure is available in eBook and paperback at
TheKureBook.com

Jaye Frances Books arc Available in
eBook and Paperback at:

JayeFrancesBooks.com

JayeFrances.com

www.ingramcontent.com/pod-product-compliance
Lightning Source LLC
Chambersburg PA
CBHW050930120626
46552CB00001B/134